Michelle Cruz Skinner, only
much longer. She understa[n]
are written with such simp[le]
with urgency the proper re[...]
ones, hardly stories, have this intensity. Take "A Modern Parable."
It's short but deadly. The author knows her American bases in the
Philippines: the bars, the beggars, the Philippine girls, the wayward
and the poor, the American servicemen, the colored and the white,
their transformation far away from home. In "In the Neon City by
the River" Michelle Skinner reveals all these. "They always stop for
us," from the mouth of an American serviceman, sums it all up.
"All Souls" fills me with nostalgia for a world I used to be a part
of. And, of course, "Balikbayan"—the tragedy of the returning native
who finds herself a stranger in her own land after a long absence.
The variety of the stories impresses and delights me. Although some
of the stories are pole apart, they are all touched with authenticity
and feeling. I think very highly of her art."

Bienvenido N. Santos, author of *Scent of Apples*

"*Balikbayan* is an excellent and convincing presentation of the ironies
and contradictions of contemporary Philippines culture, with a fine
sense of character and, particularly, visual detail."

Ian Macmillan, author of *Proud Monster*

"These are wonderful stories, and they offer rare and timeless
insights into the Philippines now and in the recent past. Rare
because Michelle Cruz Skinner is a born-and-raised Filipina but also
an American, so her vision bridges both worlds. Timeless because
we are made to care for the people in these stories, especially the
young people, and the human heart is universal. It's a remarkable
accomplishment for a first book, even for a clearly-talented writer."

Robert Shapard, editor of *Sudden Fiction*

"Faith Healer," the opening story in *Balikbayan*, was one of 54
stories selected for nationwide syndication in the 7th Annual PEN
Syndicated Fiction Project in 1988.

BALIKBAYAN

A Filipino Homecoming

Michelle Cruz Skinner

3565 Harding Avenue
Honolulu, Hawai'i 96816
phone: (808) 734-7159
fax: (808) 732-3627
e-mail: sales@besspress.com
http://www.besspress.com

Library of Congress CATALOG CARD NO: 88-70380

Skinner, Michelle Maria Cruz
      BALIKBAYAN: A Filipino Homecoming
       1.   Filipinos in the Philippines—Fiction

ISBN: 978-1-57306-290-9

Printed in the United States of America

CONTENTS

Faith Healer

I was born feet first and believed that this made me able to heal people. Grandfather seemed to believe this too. Whenever a fishbone was stuck in his throat he would come to me and have me lick my index and middle fingers and rub his throat. He was always very old to me and I remember the skin on his throat being loose and soft.

"Lolo, is it working? Is it loose?" I would ask, and he would just point at my fingers and keep trying to clear his throat. It made me feel important when he would stand before me presenting his throat to my fingers. But, I wondered what else it was that I was supposed to be able to heal people of.

Mama said I was lucky. Being born upside down, I could have died before I got out into the world. That's why I was so serious she said. Mama believed that children who had faced death in this way were either very serious or very lighthearted.

This didn't make any sense to me at the time. I knew that I didn't laugh very often, and I tended to think things over carefully. It seemed that I just didn't take life in as easy and reckless a manner as most other children. Maybe that's why I didn't really care for the company of other children.

When I was alone, I would read or draw or make up stories in my head. At Lolo's house I would mostly draw. This was because Lolo knew I liked to draw and always made sure that he had plenty of scratch paper and crayons in his study. I would pull a newspaper out of Lolo's tall stack of newspapers.

The *Bulletin Today* always had a lot of pictures, but *Manila News* was smaller and easier for me to handle. Also, their articles were shorter and used smaller, simpler words that I knew. Lolo had been a journalist until he retired. That was why he had a study and so many books and why he subscribed to so many papers and read them all. At least I thought that was why. He was proud of his reading. When he came back from the hospital, after his stroke, he tried to read a newspaper and realized that he couldn't. He cried for a long time that night. The next morning I crept downstairs and found him in his study surrounded by stacks of books and newspapers.

While he remained unable to read, he refused to see visitors. This was a problem for Mama and my aunts and uncles because Lolo had a lot of visitors who inquired after his health and wanted to wish him well. Relatives and a lot of his former coworkers came by. We lied about Lolo's health and took the cakes and candies and fruit that they brought.

Lolo soon remembered how to read and the next time we visited him I brought him a book. Mama tried to talk me out of it. "Don't waste your money. He has more than enough books." But I insisted. "You're hard-headed, like your Lolo," she said.

One night when we were at Lolo's, when I was almost asleep, I was jolted by the shrill siren of an ambulance. I ran to Mama's room crying because I thought they were coming for Lolo. It turned out to be Mang Boy, the man who lived in the little one-room house next door.

All the neighbors said he was an artist but I had never seen any of his paintings. I imagined that he kept them hidden in his house and that when he died we would finally see them. He didn't die that night.

The next day Sita, the laundrywoman, told us that he had had a heart attack when he heard on the radio that President Johnson had suffered one. That was the first that I had ever heard of President Johnson.

Lolo just said that President Johnson wasn't worth it. I believed Lolo because he knew more about President Johnson than I did. We agreed that Mang Boy was a very foolish man.

A few months later when we went to visit Lolo for his birthday he met us at the gate with a very weary and somber expression.

"Martial law has been declared," he said.

"Marshall who?" Mama said as she struggled to get out of the car. "Who's he?"

"No. Mar-tial law," Lolo pronounced carefully. "Military rule. Proclaimed by Presidential decree just this afternoon."

"Oh."

"President Johnson?" I was getting confused.

"Nooo."

"Oh." I thought about this for a minute. "Did he have another heart attack and die?" Lolo said no again and then mumbled something about how he wished somebody else would die. For the rest of the day everyone was quiet and very serious. I was sorry we had come to visit. We all went to sleep early that night.

Lolo typed in his study all the next day. He moved the phone into his study with him and made a lot of phone calls in between his typing. I sat on one side of his desk and drew pictures while he sat on the other side and typed and called people. I was the only one allowed to keep him company. He shouted at anyone else who entered.

Mama and Auntie Perla, my oldest auntie, complained about Lolo's behavior at dinner. Lolo just continued to pick at his fish.

"You could at least behave better in front of your granddaughter," Mama said. Lolo looked down at my clean plate with the utensils neatly laid across. Then he looked at me.

"Are you tired, girl?"

"Yes, Lolo."

"Give her a bath and put her to bed. But don't get her hair wet or she'll get a cold."

"Tatay, you're not listening to us!" Mama complained. Lolo finally looked at Mama.

"You're going home tomorrow aren't you?"

"Yes."

"Take her home to her father. Keep her in the American school." Lolo finished by wiping his mouth on a napkin and leaving the table. I wanted to stay in Manila with Lolo, but we left the next day as we had planned.

A few days later Daddy came home with a Filipino newspaper. Daddy always had a newspaper with him, but it was usually the *Stars and Stripes*. He seldom bought Filipino newspapers and he bought only the *Bulletin Today* when he did. This newspaper wasn't the *Bulletin Today*.

"Lorna!" he yelled as he walked in the door.

"Hi Daddy!" I called from the couch. He ignored me.

"Looornaa!"

"What?" Mama yelled from the kitchen. "I'm in here!"

"Your father is in the paper!"

My mother came running out of the kitchen with blood on her hands. "Ay Dios ko! Why? What happened?" Mama always expected news to be bad.

"What happened, Dad?"

"Just look at this!" Dad held up a page of the newspaper to Mama and pointed to an article. "He's gone and criticized our, well, your, beloved President."

Mama grabbed the paper away from Dad, smearing blood all over it as she gripped the pages tightly. It looked like the newspaper was bleeding. Or maybe Mama was. "Ay! This is... terrible!" she moaned as she read the article. "He's too old to be doing these sorts of things." I was trying to peek at the article from under her arm, but I didn't know which one she was reading. She finished the article quickly and snapped the paper to the front page to look at the masthead. "My God!"

"I know."

"This is a radical paper. They're all UP radicals!"

"The University of the Philippines is your alma mater, hon."

"Yes, but we weren't like this," my mother replied indignantly. "How did you know? You never buy this paper."

"He called me. Can you believe that?" Dad shook his head. "He called me at the office this afternoon." I didn't see anything unusual about that. Since we didn't have a telephone, Lolo always called Daddy at the office when he wanted to tell us something. "He called and told me about it, so of course I went out and bought a paper right away."

"Well, what are we going to do?" Mama groaned. She walked into the kitchen and began scrubbing her hands in the sink, trying to get the blood off. We stood behind her and watched silently. Dad didn't appear to have any answer to her question. We just listened to the water rushing over Mama's hands.

"We have to call Perlita and the others," Mama suddenly decided.

"Why do we have to call Auntie Perla," I said. "Can't we just call Lolo?" Mama brushed me away from her skirt and brushed my question aside. She ran to put on some shoes. Dad had already gone back outside. I heard the car start and then Mama ran out.

"Can I come?" I yelled at her.

"Susan will take care of you!" Mama yelled back. She climbed into the car and they drove off. Susan, the maid, dragged me away from the door and made me sit in the kitchen with her while she finished making the dinner my mother had abandoned. I remained sullen and pouted. When it came time for dinner, I refused to eat and cried instead.

Mama and Daddy came home late that night. Mama came into my room while I was lying in the dark and started packing my clothes. I watched her silently for a few moments until I could separate her body from her shadow in the dark room.

"Mama, are we going to Manila tomorrow?"

"Yes, honey. Go back to sleep."

"Is Lolo okay?"

"Go back to sleep, dear."

They carried me into the car the next morning before I was fully awake. Mama had packed some sandwiches and bananas and we had those for breakfast. We drove over the Zigzag, through the dusty little barrios and past the small towns without stopping. We reached Manila, sore and tired from the long drive, a little after noon.

After we got there things happened so quickly that it seemed like everyone was whirling around me. Auntie Perla met us at Lolo's house and then the other aunts and uncles arrived one by one bringing all their kids with them. It was hot and noisy in the house and I became grouchy.

Lolo wasn't there when we got there. Later in the evening we all went to Camp Crame where Auntie Perla said Lolo was, but I never saw him. None of us saw him. All I saw were a lot of Army men and a lot of ugly brown buildings. I didn't know if Lolo was really there or not. I hoped not because the men there didn't smile.

Daddy went back home the next day but Mama and I stayed. I really wanted to go back home. Lolo wasn't around and I hated my cousins who were so noisy and stupid. They never left me alone. And my aunts and uncles got angry at me for being unfriendly.

Lolo never came home. A week later Auntie Perla answered the telephone and screamed. We all came running and crowded around her quietly while she tried to talk to the person on the other end of the phone. She was frantically pulling out drawers and flinging open the doors of cabinets searching for something. Mama passed her a small notebook and a pen and, still listening to the phone, she wrote something down. We all left after that and drove for almost an hour through the heavy diesel smog of Manila traffic until we came to a large, dirty white building in a strange part of town.

It was a hospital. The nurse took us up to Lolo's room and then left us as quickly as possible. Lolo lay flat on a narrow bed with a white sheet stretched taut across him pinning him to the mattress. Even if the sheet hadn't been there, I don't think he could have moved.

His skin wasn't the wax-paper thinness that I remembered. It was almost transparent now. I could see not only the dark blue veins on his neck, but also tiny blood vessels. The skin on his neck looked even more loose and wrinkled than I remembered. He never opened his eyes, but just kept sleeping. I was afraid to touch him he looked so weak.

The nurses tried to make us leave, but there were too many of us to throw out. So, we stayed there for the night, sleeping in the few chairs in the room and out in the hallway. I wanted to stay awake, but I couldn't.

When I woke up the next morning, someone had already taken Lolo away. I believed that I could heal people, but I hadn't been able to help him at all. I found out that all I could do was remove fish-bones from people's throats. And only Lolo truly believed that I could do that.

They Don't Give Scholarships to Artists

The rich ladies, they don't give scholarships to artists. You know the scholarships, the ones for high school. Every year they give them to sixth graders. This year I'm grade six, so I apply.

These women, they're from a benevolent association. That's what it says on the application. Mrs. Bautista, my homeroom teacher, she says to fill one out. "You're a good student, Niño. You should apply." I says I don't know. The next day she gives me the form.

I want to go to high school. But if I do, I can't work. I don't know if my parents would like that. But I hear that one boy, he received a scholarship and now he graduated and is in college. I think, I can do that. So I apply.

My mother, she signs the form. She says she will tell my father later. I take the application to Mrs. Perez in the office. She is the school secretary. She doesn't like me, I don't know why, and asks why my father doesn't sign. But Mrs. Bautista, who accompanies me, says it doesn't matter. I need only one signature. So, Mrs. Perez, the sourpuss, has to take my application.

Later that week, the principal tells Mrs. Bautista and Mrs. Bautista tells me the interviewers will come next week. My appointment is after lunch hour. I don't want to miss my appointment, so I don't leave the school. Because I don't go home, I have no lunch, so I'm very hungry when I speak with the interviewers.

Gerardo Banay and I meet with the interviewers together. Gerardo is a smart, fat boy from my homeroom class. I helped him once on a project because he cannot draw. I see him outside the room where the interviewers are and I think, I don't know why he is here because his father has a job. But I guess anybody can apply.

He walks in first, then me. When they see me, the ladies stares. People always stares at me. I says to the ladies it is because I had polio that my leg is like this. They nod like they understand.

They ask about our favorite subjects. I says I like art and physical education. One of the ladies looks at me as if this is not true. But I tell the truth. Gerardo lies. He says he likes mathematics and English. Gerardo hates mathematics. He does like English.

Then they asks about our families. I tell them my mother is a laundrywoman and my father is a vendor. He sells things. I have five brothers and three sisters. Gerardo says his mother does not work. And his father works in a restaurant. He has two sisters.

The ladies writes everything down. Then they asks us what we want to be when we get older. Gerardo says he wants to be a civil engineer. I know he is lying. He does not know what a civil engineer is. I don't know. The women smile and asks him what a civil engineer is. He doesn't answer.

They asks me the question. I says, "I want to be an artist." The oldest lady, she asks, "Why do you want to do that?" I says that I like it. One of the others, she asks me what kind of artist I want to be and I says I want to paint. The third lady asks me how I will make money. I says I will paint. Two of them, they asks and asks the same questions so I don't think they like my answer.

10

I tell them I am a very good painter and I can show them one of my projects. One of the ladies, the one who asked what kind of artist I want to be, she wants to see it. The other ladies says they have no time. They have to see many more students and they smile and says "thank you for coming."

A week later, during the morning announcements after the national anthem, the principal tells all the students that Elena Salcedo will receive the scholarship. The ladies are there and they present Elena with an award. Elena is scared and says quietly that she wants to continue her studies and be a nurse.

I am not going to school, so my mother will not have to tell my father anything about the scholarship. I will be a vendor and sell my own paintings.

Simbang Gabi

Early Christmas morning a fire started behind the rickety shack that stood in the small, weed-filled lot between our house and the house of Doctor de Guzman. Almost everyone was at Simbang Gabi, Midnight Mass, and the two of us who started it didn't do anything to stop it. The fire was very bright and burned strongly for almost half an hour. Fortunately, there was very little physical damage done. It blackened part of a wall and scorched the ground around it. I remember that it did more good than bad. A lot went up in the smoke from that fire.

The fire occurred on the land being illegally occupied by Mang Lito and his family. The owner of the lot lived in Manila and hadn't visited Olongapo in years. He never knew about the family living on his land and no one really cared enough to tell him. It was a small, rubble-strewn lot, once the site of a church, some of the older residents claimed, bordered by the two houses, the street and a fetid canal choked with garbage. Mang Lito's shack of corrugated aluminum, large pieces of plywood and heavy cardboard sat close to the street on what was left of the old building foundation.

Mang Lito and his family of ten came one sweltering March day, a few days before summer vacation and my fifteenth birthday, and promptly set up house in the vacant lot. Poor people like them were always setting up crude houses wherever they could find some vacant land. There were three other shacks on our street alone. No one paid much attention

13

to the newcomers until they started to host noisy gatherings at which the guests played cards, gambled and sometimes became very drunk on the strong cane liquor Mang Lito made.

Many nights I lay in bed listening to them insult each other, laugh raucously, fight and play their radio too loudly. Sometimes, overcome by curiosity, I would stand on my bed and peer out my window, over the wall, and into the lot below. People were always spilling out of the doorways so that there were more card players outside than inside.

I don't know why I was so attracted to that collection of drunks, gamblers, and fighters. I never wanted to meet any of them, but I loved to watch them.

After tolerating a month of their rambunctious gatherings, a group of citizens persuaded the local pseudo-police, the Baranggay Tanod, to pay a visit to the family and express the neighborhood's displeasure. This, like many other things the Tanod did, met with little success.

Claring, Mang Lito's wife, was ready for them. Boyet, a young boy who was hopelessly infatuated with their only daughter, Memet, rushed breathlessly into their house a few minutes before the Baranggay Tanod arrived. Seconds later, the drunks and card players rushed out of the house, tripping over each other in their eagerness to get out of Claring's way. When the Tanod arrived, she and Mang Lito were sitting quietly on the rough, wooden benches in front of their home sipping Coca-Colas.

For about two weeks after that incident, their home was fairly quiet. My mother was disappointed that they hadn't been chastised more strongly or been arrested. She worried that our neighbors and the "hoodlums" they entertained would sneak into our yard through the large, jagged crack in the wall that separated our houses and make off with some of the things she stored in the old storage cabinet in back of the house. There was really nothing worth stealing back there, but Mother didn't trust anybody who was poor. I suspected that she was one of the upstanding citizens who had protested so loudly and continuously that the Tanod had finally been forced out of its characteristic indolence.

She found our neighbors' way of life shocking and a black smear on the good name of our neighborhood. Now, I think that she was probably at least partly right, but I didn't know much about reputations then.

"Those people are hayop! Animals! They corrupt the young men! Something should be done about them! And that girl!"

"That girl" was Memet who had never actually done anything scandalous as far as the neighborhood knew, but who attracted such a horde of young men that people gossiped anyway. I admired her. She possessed a haughty air and a playful, cruel manner that could cut anyone down. She always said exactly what she felt, something I could never do. I enjoyed watching her entertain the crowd of admirers who gathered at her house.

Most of the time she joked around, conversed and flirted with them. Some days she ignored them. This angered them, but they seemed to forget about it the next day when she was talking to them again. She was beautiful, in a way that I wanted to be beautiful, with dark, shiny hair and large, deep brown eyes that moved constantly, impatiently from object to object.

Mother thought she was too dark. "She looks Moro," she said, in reference to the dark Muslims of the southern Philippines. I didn't look Moro at all. I was very pale, having inherited my father's Filipino-Chinese complexion and my mother's Filipino-Spanish one. My long, black hair made me look even paler, which I didn't like. Pale skin, though, was something that most people coveted. It was very fashionable.

When Mother found out that I had been named queen for the baranggay, the neighborhood, Christmas pageant, she felt vindicated in her opinion. She smiled happily, across the dinner table at me.

"I told you Clara; you're very beautiful," Mother said between bites of fish. But I had heard her say such polite things to too many people to believe her. Besides, I was sure everyone in the neighborhood thought Memet should have been queen. But everyone, especially the pageant committee, must have known she couldn't afford a proper dress.

"You'll need to have a dress made."
I stared down at the fish slathered with tomatoes and onions that lay sprawled on my plate.

"We'll make you a beautiful dress and you'll be the best-looking queen ever."

Father nodded happily, as if he agreed, but his attention was focused on the ledger by his plate that informed him his animal feed business was making money.

That night I heard Memet and her mother Claring arguing in hushed voices outside my window. They stood by the mango tree ignoring the hooting and hollering from inside their home. The full moon cast a pale, silver light on their faces, making them look like pictures of unknown relatives from an old family album. They conversed earnestly and frantically. Even though I wasn't supposed to be watching, I felt that I belonged there, that what they were arguing about somehow involved me. Finally, Memet stormed into the house and left Claring standing alone with a pained expression on her face.

The next day I was walking home from school alone because my friend Gemma, Dr. deGuzman's daughter, had to stay after school for a meeting. I didn't really mind. Most of the time I preferred being alone to being with other people, even with Gemma. We were best friends, but we weren't really very close. We were just friends because we were neighbors and went to the same private school—St. Ann's. We got along well enough and my mother was pleased with her. We would probably forget about each other once we left Olongapo for college in Manila. The thought really didn't bother me. I walked on the dusty, unpaved road past the baranggay high school, the public school.

"Clara," a voice behind me called. I was startled to see Memet walking right behind me. I smiled uncertainly. "I hear you're going to be queen." Her voice sounded strained.

"Yes," I mumbled. Why did she have to remind me? We stood in an awkward silence while she stared at me. Unable to take her gaze, I dropped my head and looked at the ground. "Everyone expected it."

I stared at the tops of my dust-covered white shoes. I could feel the sharp gravel of the road poking through the soles and into my feet. My feet hurt. I wished Memet would go away, so I wouldn't have to talk to her. I couldn't think of anything else to say. Finally, she left me, her slippers slapping against the gravel as she walked to her house.

When I got home I found Mother out on the porch with Sita, our maid. They were hanging up the parols, the colorful, star-shaped, paper Christmas lanterns that were supposed to represent the Star of Bethlehem. "Hello, Clara. You want to help us?" Mother said, her tone implying I was expected to help. "We're going to hang up the lights next and then we can have merienda." I didn't really want to wait any longer to eat merienda, my stomach was already twisting and complaining, but I had to. With the three of us working, it didn't take very long to hang up the lights. Soon Mother and I were sitting at the dining room table eating the bread and guava jam that Sita served us. "We can set up the Nativity scene and the Christmas tree tomorrow," Mother decided, and dragged me out to the dressmaker's to be fitted for a gown for the pageant.

I brought along a picture of the gown I wanted and Mother brought along some white, eyelet material she had purchased that morning. The material was not very pretty. "Nanay, why did you buy that?"

"It will look good on you," she replied.

Mother often bought me things that she wanted. That was the way she did things. The curtains and bedspread in my room were yellow because that was my mother's favorite color, instead of blue, which was my favorite. I think now, that maybe she forgot what I liked.

Gemma came over that night to study for the Filipino history test with me. "Have you seen Clara's gown?" my mother gushed as soon as Gemma walked in the door. Mother knew that Gemma couldn't have seen the gown yet. She made me run and get the picture, then described in full detail the material and the little changes she had made to the original design. I sat sulking in one corner of the living room. "Clara is so excited about it," Mother concluded happily.

I tried to change the subject. "Are you going to the basketball game this weekend?"

"Of course. It's for the city championship." Gemma smiled. "We might even win."

"Do you need a ride?"

"Well, my mother was going to drop me off."

Mother joined in the conversation. "Tell her not to worry. Clara and I are going, so you can ride with us." She seemed to forget about the gown and left Gemma and I to our studying.

That Saturday night Gemma was late getting to our house, and we were a half-hour late for the game, which was to be played in a park halfway across town. She apologized profusely and I was upset but pretended not to be. Mother didn't mind that Gemma was late since the game didn't matter much to her anyway. She just liked driving around in our new blue Toyota Corolla. To be honest, the game didn't mean that much to me either. I just didn't like to be late for anything.

We lost by thirty points to the Gordon Heights Barangay High School. Memet's school. After the game, I saw Memet standing by the edge of the road. She was waiting for a blue jeepney, a cross between a jeep and a small bus. The blue jeepneys were the only ones that went into our area of town. Memet stared coolly at us for a moment. Mother saw Memet and so did Gemma but none of us said anything. We drove off leaving her standing under the harsh, yellow streetlight talking to some boys from her school.

On the way home, Mother broached the subject of college. "I really think you should talk to your cousin Erlinda about De Salles. We could afford it and from what she's said, it sounds like a very good school."

"Yes, Nanay." I was only half-listening. I stared out at the small stores and the small houses crowded together that zipped past my window. Mother continued talking. We passed a group of people gathered around a sari-sari store drinking and smoking. As we drove past, I could hear their laughter and a few notes of the guitar that one of them was playing.

"Maria Clara are you listening to me?"

"Yes, Nanay." I hated it when she called me by my full name. Maria Clara was the ideal, obedient, demure, beautiful Filipina. Mother always hoped I would live up to the ideal. She is probably still hoping. As a child, I had wanted to be like Maria Clara, but by the age of fifteen I had decided there were many other things I would rather be.

"Clara, I think you should call your cousin Erlinda when she comes home for Christmas. De Salles sounds like a good school. Don't you agree, Gemma? Or Marymount. But I don't want you going to the University of the Philippines. The students there are always causing trouble."

De Salles and Marymount? Those were exclusive, very expensive schools and the students were likely to be like my cousin Erlinda and her Manila friends: rich, conceited and always very fashionably dressed. I would much rather go to the University of the Philippines. UP students were supposed to be radicals. They would probably be much more interesting.

"Erlinda's majoring in mass communications there. I hear

they have a good mass comm. ...." Mother slammed on the brakes and we lurched forward in our seats. "Those stupid jeepney drivers!"

I caught a glimpse of Memet sitting in the back of the blue jeepney as it sped off down the dark street. She seemed to be smiling.

"Did you see that? Thos jeepney drivers should learn how to drive!" Mother ranted and raved about the jeepney all the way home. I was actually grateful because she forgot about Erlinda and De Salles and mass comm. What kind of major was mass comm. anyway? The thought bothered me as I lay in bed trying to sleep. Mang Lito's house was quiet that night and I didn't see Memet or any of her family out in the yard.

The next night, though, was different. Mang Lito's house was crowded again. Hidden by the darkness in my room, I watched them. Card players streamed out of the front and back doors and Memet floated among them flirting with some and ignoring others. Two men, who didn't appear very drunk but were apparently very angry, got into a fist fight in the back of the house. Other card players joined in and in the melee that followed, Mang Lito's still was knocked over and somehow caught on fire. The fire was quickly put out and the two men unceremoniously dumped in the canal. Memet appeared very amused by it all. So was I.

The next morning she appeared to be in a good mood and walked as far as her school with me. She talked about the latest exploits of her favorite movie star and I listened eagerly. "My cousin Erlinda knows him," I said proudly. Memet looked at me skeptically. "Well, she's met him before. I have a picture of the two of them together."

"Really?" Memet now sounded very interested.

"Yes. Would you like to see it? You can come over to my house after school." I was sorry as soon as I said it. Mother would not want Memet at our house, and she would not be very friendly to her.

"Okay," she agreed. It was too late to retract the invitation. At least she was dressed well today.

That afternoon, I tried to get us into the house as quietly as possible, but not much every slipped past my mother. "Clara is that you?" she yelled down from her bedroom as we were climbing the stairs.

"Yes, Nanay!"

She appeared at the top of the stairs and surveyed the scene below her.

"Hello, Memet." Mother smiled in a perfectly polite manner.

"Hello, ma'am." Memet imitated her tone of voice and her stiff smile. I had to stifle an urge to laugh. Mother turned her attention to me.

"Clara, go see what's on your bed." She sounded excited as she always was when she bought me something that she liked. Usually she got me frilly dresses in pink or yellow that I hated and then she expected me to wear them.

I tried to look excited too. "All right, Nanay." I hurried up the stairs with Memet following me.

Lying on my bed was my gown for the Christmas pageant. It was not exactly what I had asked for. The neckline wasn't a scoop neckline as I had shown the dressmaker, but more of a straight line from sleeve to sleeve. And the sleeves were a subtle variation of the traditional butterfly sleeves. The bodice was fitted, with a large, pink satin rose sewn onto the waist. It had a full, long skirt that covered the bottom half of the bedspread and spilled over onto the floor. "It's beautiful," Memet whispered. "Can I try it on?"

"Well, um ..." Not that I didn't want to let her try it on, but I was just surprised that she had asked. I couldn't recall her ever asking me for anything. I glanced nervously out my bedroom door, but Mother had gone downstairs. Quietly, I closed the door.

"Go ahead. Try it on." Memet took off her faded blue

school skirt and white blouse and eagerly pulled the gown over her head. She flailed around for a few moments trying to get her head through the sea of fabric that made up the skirt. Finally, she had it on and I zipped her up. I made her stand on the bed, so she could see herself in the mirror over my dresser. She twirled around happily and struck a few poses like those she had seen in the fashion pages of the movie magazines. The fitted bodice was a little loose, but she looked beautiful in it anyway.

In the middle of one of her poses, a reflection in the mirror caught her attention. She whirled around to face the window and peered out. Then she looked back in the mirror and finally at me. "That's your window I can see from our house." She sounded surprised. Or maybe accusing?

"Yes," I mumbled nervously and averted my gaze. The afternoon heat suddenly felt very oppressive and I could feel the little rivers of sweat trickling down my back, my arms, and my legs. Memet laughed. Startled, I glanced back up at her smiling face.

Still smiling, she took off the gown and put her own clothes back on. "Try it on," Memet said. "It's your gown." She made me get up on the bed too and laughed delightedly as I struck a few poses. Mother walked in just then. We instantly quieted down. She glanced suspiciously at us as if trying to decipher what had happened in her absence.

"You look beautiful, dear," she finally said to me. "Now come downstairs. Erlinda is here. She just got in from Manila yesterday and I invited her over for merienda this afternoon." Mother looked at Memet. "Shouldn't you be getting home? Your mother might be worried about you."

"Yes, ma'am," Memet replied politely. "I do have to be getting home." She smiled politely, retrieved her notebook from the dresser and headed downstairs with me right behind her.

"Clara!" Erlinda rose from her seat in the living room to

greet me. She hesitated when she noticed Memet in her faded and ill-fitting public school uniform. Memet ignored her and continued out the door.

"Hi, Lin." I tried to sound enthusiastic. "I'll be right back." Memet was already halfway out the front gate by then. "Memet!" She stopped and waited impatiently for me. "I'm sorry," I said.

"I know," she replied with a conspiratorial smile and walked off. I suddenly remembered that I hadn't shown her the picture of her favorite movie star.

Erlinda was her usual gossipy self. She regaled us with stories about parties and debuts and famous people she had met. She showed off her new Christian Dior blouse and the gold necklace one of her boyfriends had given her. We also heard about her diet when she politely refused the pastries that Mother had set out for our merienda. She didn't talk about De Salles or mass comm. except when Mother specifically asked her about it.

That evening there was an impromptu dance in Mang Lito's backyard. It began with some men playing guitar and singing, but eventually the crowd grew tired of them and someone turned on a radio. With Madonna and Sharon Cuneta blaring loudly in the background, they danced and drank. For a few moments I saw Memet. She was staring at my bedroom window and I was sure that she could see right into the darkness to me perched on the bed. She smiled and then she was caught up again in the crowd and disappeared.

The Christmas pageant was in two more days and our house was being made ready for it. Mother had invited quite a few people over for a small party after the pageant and before Midnight Mass. The two parish priests had been invited along with all three of the pageant princesses, one of whom was Gemma, and their parents, as well as the members of the pageant committee, Erlinda and her family, and some other people whom I didn't know very well. So, for the past two days the kitchen had been busy with women chopping, mixing, grating, scaling, frying, and baking.

I wasn't too thrilled about the idea of a party because I wanted to stay for the dance that was to be held after the pageant program was over. Memet had promised to introduce me to some of the boys she knew. Mother, however, insisted on having a party and insisted that I help with the preparations. "We're doing this for you," she would remind me whenever I tried to get out of helping.

The day of the Christmas pageant, Mother took me to the hairdresser. I hated going to the hairdresser's because he would always try to cut my long hair. That day, though, he insisted on piling it high on top of my head and teasing it. The teasing was painful and I was getting depressed just thinking about how I was ever going to get all the tangles out of my hair. Then, despite my objections and my attempts to get out of the chair, he drenched my hair in hairspray. Afterwards, he did my nails in a shade of pink that he thought would match the satin rose on my dress. The nail polish looked better in the bottle than on my nails. I felt very artificial and left the beauty salon miserable.

The makeup for the pageant was the worse. It was so thick and stiff. As I sat on the platform, under the strong lights, with the princesses and all of the honored guests, I was sure my makeup was sliding off with the numerous little beads of sweat rolling down my face. The program seemed to take forever as person after person sang and danced and gave speeches.

It looked like the whole neighborhood had packed into the Gordon Heights Barangay High School field. Some of them weren't paying attention to the program at all. They wandered around the fringes of the crowd talking and eating the Christmas sweets sold by vendors with pushcarts who had flocked to this event like flies.

Somewhere in the crowd was Memet, but, try as I might, I couldn't see her. Mother, of course, was right in the front row snapping pictures. Father was with her, looking completely unmoved by all the activity.

The program was finally over and we rushed home in the blue Toyota Corolla. It didn't take the guests very long to arrive. Within half an hour the house was filled to overflowing with guests. When it seemed that most everyone was there, Father Garcia, the older of the two parish priests, led the whole crowd in a grace before the meal. Father Garcia liked long sermons and long prayers and the simple grace before a meal was for him a drawn-out affair. The guests seemed relieved when it was finally over and they eagerly lined up at the table for the food.

There was stuffed fish, noodles, lumpia, chicken adobo, vegetables sautéed in fish sauce, pork stew, and lots of rice. For dessert there was fruit salad with coconut milk, leche flan with caramel sauce and various pastries. Everyone wandered around the house with paper plates eating, drinking sodas, and dropping little bits of food on the floor. The smell of the various foods was overwhelming. That, combined with the still, moist night air and the musky sweat of too many bodies in too small a space, was making me a little nauseated.

I stood by the dining room table drinking the tea that Sita had made to settle my stomach down. Father Garcia, who was making yet another trip to the table, stopped to chat with me, remarking, as he had on many occasions, on what a well-behaved and pleasant girl I was. "You should consider the religious life, Clara." I dropped my cup of tea. The brown liquid ran all over the white tablecloth, devouring all the little pink embroidered flowers in its path.

As Sita was cleaning up the mess, I excused myself and took refuge in my room. The gown felt like a dead weight, and I peeled it frantically from my sweating body. I kicked it away from me and it lay sprawled in one corner of the floor. The makeup felt itchy, like it was crawling on my face, so I scrubbed it all off and lay on my bed in my underwear.

The sound of music from next door seeped through the curtains of my room. It was Christmas music blaring from a cheap radio. The tinny sound drifted in my window along with cheap cigarette smoke and the laughter of a party. I peered out the window and saw that a small party was indeed in progress over at Mang Lito's house.

Quickly, I threw my favorite blue cotton dress on. In the back of my closet I found a pair of comfortable, old, white sandals lying on the floor. I picked them up and was about to leave when the dress, lying in one dark corner of the floor, caught my eye. I plucked it from the floor and rolled it into a tight ball. With the dress under one arm and the sandals in hand, I sneaked out the kitchen door. Sita saw me, but I gave her a pleading look and she calmly returned to her cooking.

I couldn't go out the front gate because everyone sitting out on the porch would see me. Instead I decided to climb through the crack in the wall between our house and Mang Lito's. Mother had attempted to barricade the crack by having large pieces of wood and other debris piled on our side of the wall. But it wasn't a very high pile and I climbed over it easily and jumped down to the other side. I put my sandals on and hesitantly walked around to the front of the house. I hoped I wouldn't run into any of Mang Lito's drunk friends.

Memet was sitting out in the front talking to a group of young men. They eyed me suspiciously as I approached. I felt nervous, being among all these people whom I knew but had never had anything to do with. When Memet saw me approach she excused herself and walked over to me.

"Hello," she said in a coolly polite manner as she stood stiffly before me.

"Hello," I replied nervously. I shifted the gown to my other arm. "Can I join you?"

Memet relaxed and gave me a little smile. "Yes." She pointed at the recognizable bundle under my arm. "Why did you bring that?"

"I don't know. I guess I thought I could get rid of it. I just didn't want to see it around anymore."

Memet nodded. "What do you want to do with it?"

I considered her question as I glanced around at the men waving their cards in the smoky air and passing bottles of liquor around.

"Burn it." I was surprised. My voice sounded so loud. It seemed to cut through the smoke and noise around us to hang strongly, conclusively in the air. Memet looked at me uncertainly. "Burn it," I repeated confidently.

Memet released my arm and walked up to one of the boys she had been talking with. She returned with a box of matches. She led me around the back of the house, right up to the jagged crack in the wall.

We gathered dry leaves from the ground around the mango tree. Memet found a few newspapers by the back door of her house. The few stunted bushes by the canal yielded some dried branches. Methodically, we gathered our materials aided by the light of the moon and the many lights on in our house and in Memet's.

When the pyre was completed, I placed the gown on top of it. "Wait a moment," Memet said and ran to her father's still and returned with a bottle. She sprinkled the contents on the dress. "Okay. Now light it." I struck three matches and laid them in different areas of the pyre.

We sat on the wall. The matches burned weakly. One flickered, glowed and died out. We waited anxiously. Finally, a flame shot up, suddenly ignited by the alcohol, and blazed brightly. The fire greedily devoured the twigs and leaves and worked up to the gown. Soon there were huge, glowing holes in the fabric. Memet and I sat, arm in arm, in the jagged crack in the wall, transfixed by the tongues of flame glowing in the darkness. The spell was broken by the sudden crack and ringing of metal in the air.

"What's that?" I cried, startled by the sudden noise.

27

"Simbang Gabi," Memet replied. "Those are the church bells." The bells reverberated through the air. Each peal was strong and crisp as the flames which shot up higher and higher to a crescendo that devoured the last of the gown.

Memet and I smiled and then giggled and finally laughed. We laughed for a long, long time that night in front of our altar of flames.

At the Corner of EDSA

"**I** swear I didn't see him," the young American man repeated for the third time. The police officer still was not listening. He was busy yelling threats at the excited crowd that eagerly clustered around the scene of the accident. He was a wide, strongly-built man who exuded the authority of his position. The crowd was wary of him, but continued to surge inward toward the sprawled body of the young boy.

"Patay kaya?" Dead or not? The question buzzed around.

A woman knelt over the body of the boy. She wailed and pulled at her hair, her bayong of groceries overturned. Sitaw, tokwa, tomatoes, spilled out of the bag and into the crowd, were trampled and mashed into the concrete.

"Pinatay niya! Pinatay niya!" the women wailed.

The policeman, feeling that the crowd was somewhat under control, addressed the young, blond man standing helplessly before him. "What happened?" Immediately a chorus of voices from the crowd answered his question.

"Alam mo, blind turn kasi it ...."

"Hindi tumitingin ...."

"Nag spee-speed ...."

The policeman bellowed at the crowd. "Oy! Siya ang tinatanongan ko! If I want your opinion I'll ask for it!"

The voices died down to a loud murmur. Within the crowd opinions were being exchanged as to the cause, the effect, and the outcome of the accident. Some felt that the boy, being impulsive and careless as youngsters are, had not looked before he crossed. Others were positive that the young American man had killed the boy with his reckless speeding. Almost everyone was sure that a lot of money would have to be paid by the American.

"Okay," the policeman began again. "What happened?"

"Pinatay niya! Pinatay niya!" the woman kneeling over the boy wailed. Curiosity rippled through the crowd. Who was she? The boy's mother, aunt, grandmother?

The policeman calmed her. "Huwag kayo mag alala, lola. Dadating na ang ambulance." He knew the boy wasn't dead. He could see his chest rising and falling in shallow breaths. Also, there wasn't any blood. Of course that could mean internal bleeding, but the policeman wasn't going to worry about it. That was a problem for the hospital.

He turned again to the young American. "How did this happen?"

The young man shifted nervously from foot to foot. "I was making a turn onto EDSA, and I looked real carefully before I turned—all I saw was a few people by the side of the road—anyway, I was making this turn, after looking both ways of course to make sure the road was clear ...." He clenched and unclenched his fists and wiggled his fingers around as he talked. "And then I felt this bump like the car had just hit a real bad pothole. That's what I thought it was, a bad pothole. Because the streets are so bad, you know." The crowd murmured its agreement. Potholes were a big problem for drivers in this part of the city. Down at their feet the woman's wailing had died into steady crying.

"Well, it's rainy season," the policeman explained.

"Oh, I'm not saying all the streets are bad or anything. It's just that's what I thought it was. And then all these people started crowding around my car and knocking at the windows. I got a little scared. I mean, it's not a good time to be in Manila and all."

"Manila is perfectly safe," the policeman said, defending

his city. A few people in the crowd hooted derisively. The policeman glared at the crowd and they quieted down. "Probably more safe than your New York City."

"I'm not from New York City," the young American politely corrected him.

"Where is your residence?"

"Chicago, Illinois."

"No. I mean where are you residing here?"

"Well, um, I'm with the Peace Corps."

"Where are you residing?" The policeman was getting irritable. Couldn't this Americano answer a simple question like that?

"With Father Roxas of San Sebastian Church. Actually, I work in Baguio with the Igorots. I'm just in Manila for a short break."

The policeman tried again. "Where is the residence of Father Roxas?" Meanwhile the crowd was buzzing with the news. A Peace Corps boy. Catolico perhaps? A good Christian boy anyway. Not like those spoiled Americano brats whose fathers were embassy or big business. Truly a nice boy. So clean cut, look. None of those dirty little mustaches. Ey, what's wrong with mustaches, auntie?

At their feet, the woman's sobbing increased. The crowd's sympathies wavered. Look at the poor woman. Must be her son. Where's the ambulance? This boy's going to be dead by the time it gets here. He is dead. No, he's not. Look. May as well be—probably injured for life. You've read about these things.

The woman's sobs turned into loud hiccups as she tried to catch her breath. "Ikaw!" She pointed at the young American. "Ikaw ang pumatay kay Nanding!" She began crying again.

Nanding. The police officer noted this one concrete fact down on his pad of paper. So that was the boy's name. Or his nickname at least. Close enough for now.

"Ikaw ang pumatay!" the woman wailed again. She refused

31

to believe that the boy was not dead. She turned her red and swollen face to the policeman. "Hindi kasi tumitingin ang 'Kano."

The woman began to tell her story. "Tumitingin kami at wala naman kaming nakita, kaya tumawid kami." Voices joined in from the crowd. Yes, it was just as she said. There was nothing coming when they had started to cross the street. Then you all must be blind, other voices accused. Because the car could clearly be seen approaching the corner. Impossible, it's a blind curve. You can't see anything coming. Only if you're standing by the Coconut Planters Bank is it a blind curve. And where were you standing? In the middle of the street?

The policeman bellowed at the crowd again. "Pakialamero!" He was getting tired of everyone sticking their noses into this business and answering for the two people involved. Even if the two people involved were doing a poor job of answering for themselves.

He decided to try the American again. "Where is the residence of Father Roxas?" He stood with pen poised over his notepad.

"San Sebastian Church," the American replied simply.

"And what is the address of this church?" The policeman tried not to show his exasperation.

"Well, ..." The young man paused in thought. "On Diaz Boulevard near Goldilocks Bakery. It's a couple miles over that way." He waved his hand vaguely in the direction he was speaking of.

The policeman decided to change his questioning. "Do you have the telephone number?"

The American man dug in his pockets. "Yes. Here it is." He waved a small scrap of paper in the officer's face and promptly dropped it. It fluttered to the ground and landed on the squashed and juicy remains of a tomato. He picked it up carefully and wiped it on the leg of his jeans. "You can still read it." He held it up again and the policeman took down the number.

"What is your name?"

"Ian."

"What?"

"Ian." The young man repeated it slowly. The policeman still looked confused. "It means John. Most people her call me John." The policeman wrote down "Jon."

"Surname?" the officer asked.

"Surname?"

"Yes. Surname. Family name."

"Oh. McDonough."

"Like the hamburger?"

"No. McDonough." The American man emphasized the last syllable. "M-C-D-O-N-O-U-G-H."

Strange name, everyone in the crowd agreed. It isn't very American. These Americanos. They don't use Christian names. He said his name was John. Isn't that Christian? No, he said his name was In or Een. Yan. Oy, it smells around here! It's the vegetables.

The boy stirred. Upon seeing this the woman kneeling over him renewed her cries. "Oy, Lola." The policeman tried to hush her. "Eto na ang ambulancia."

The ambulance, sirens wailing and red lights flashing, came around the disputed corner and pulled in front of the crowd. Men in long, white coats jumped out and immediately set upon the boy. Sunlight gleamed off the shiny steel instruments with which they probed for the boy's vital signs.

People came running from around the neighborhood, attracted by the noise and lights. They pushed at the edge of the crowd, trying to get a view of the proceedings. The boy was lifted into the ambulance on a stretcher. Close behind him was the sobbing woman who clung to one of the emergency medical technicians. The American man reluctantly got into the police officer's battered white jeep after being assured that his car—it wasn't really his, he tried to explain; he had borrowed it from Father Roxas—would be towed to a garage near the police station.

What's going on? the newcomers on the edge of the crowd asked. What happened?

Ay nako! Where have you been? You missed everything.

Taglish

"Kumusta! Kumusta po sa inyong lahat at welcome back! Today marami tayong prizes para sa mga lucky contestants natin. But, before we start, gusto ko munang e-introduce ang atin guest host. Ladies and gentlemen: si Mr. Herman Hernandez!"

"Hello, Marylou!"

"Hi, Uncle Hermie."

"O, good afternoon ho sa inyong lahat."

"O, now that you're here, puede na tayong mag umpisa."

"Okay! ... Our first contestant today is Miss Veronica Santos!"

"Hello Veronica, and where are you from?"

"I am ... ma'am."

"Puede mo bang e-repeat iyon Veronica?"

"I am from Caloocan ma'am."

"Miss Veronica Santos from Caloocan! O, ready ka na ba Veronica? Marami tayong prizes today folks. Hindi ba, Uncle Hermie?"

"Oo. Okay, Veronica, is there anything na gusto mong sabihin sa mga friends at family mo?"

"Opo, Uncle Hermie. Gusto ko pong mag-pa Happy Birthday sa akin nanay at hello to all the people in East Caloocan High School."

"Ah, high school ka pa pala!"

"Opo."

"Well, Marylou, what is the first game?"

35

"Uncle Hermie, our first game is the spelling bee!"

"O, maybe e-explain mo muna kay Veronica."

"Okay! In the spelling bee there are five words sa board namin. Kailangan e-choose mo iyon two correctly-spelled words. Kung tama ang choices mo, you win: a five hundred peso gift certificate at Rustans! ... Ready Veronica?"

"Yes, ma'am."

"Okay! You have ninety seconds to choose the two correctly-spelled words! Begin!"

"Ahhhh ...."

"Sixty seconds!"

"Ammm ... mathematician?"

"Thirty seconds."

"... serious ...."

"10987654321! The two correct words are ... Uncle Hermie?"

"Mathematician and lounge."

"I'm sorry, Veronica. You didn't win the gift certificate, pero Uncle Hermie will tell you what you won."

"Yes, Veronica. You have won two cases of Nissin's Instant Oriental Noodles. For playtime, snacktime, anytime! 'Pinakamalinamnam!' And a Federated Electric Fan with three speed settings. 'Masarap na mahangin.'"

"Thank you Uncle Hermie! At thank you rin kay Veronica Santos of Caloocan! We'll be back after these messages!"

The Television Man

Hesus pounded on the stubborn, rusty nail. He managed to lodge it about a quarter inch deeper into the wood before sitting back to rest. Nene glanced up from the comic book she was reading and shook her head. Hesus wiped the sweat from his face with his faded red handkerchief, then shoved the handkerchief back into the pocket of his old jeans and resumed pounding.

The work was going slowly, much slower than Hesus had expected. He worried that he might not have the cross ready by tomorrow.

In between the short rests he took, the chickens could be heard clucking agitatedly at him in the little corner where they had taken refuge from the two intruders. Even Nene clucked at him in irritation. She had allowed him to work on the cross in the cool, dark chicken coop under her family's house. But, his constant noise was annoying her and the chickens, which consequently weren't laying any eggs. Hesus crouched over his cross, oblivious to the ill-feeling that hung almost tangibly in the thick, wet air.

Sweat glistened on his arms, shoulders and back and on the wood that lay before him. The sweat trickled in tiny rivulets down to the small of his back, forming a slick sheen there. Beads of sweat burst from his forehead to drop onto the wood of the cross.

The hammer Hesus used was old and rusty as were the nails. Only the wood was new. Rather than scavenging for some

37

scrap lumber as Nene had urged him to, Hesus had spent nearly all of the meager earnings from his occasional jobs for some rich, reddish-brown narra wood from the lumberyard in town. Not only had the wood been expensive, but the cost of hauling it to her home in the jeepney had also been high.

"You're crazy!" Nene had said when she discovered how much he had spent. But he had stubbornly defended his purchases. "There will be so many people here for the celebration. I have to be seen. That's the only way I'll find my father."

"Maybe he doesn't want to be found," Nene had suggested. And when he chose to ignore her: "He doesn't even know you're alive!" Hesus had refused to listen to her and had insisted on making the cross; Nene had refused to help and left him awkwardly balancing the long beams in front of her house, wondering where he should go.

Hesus couldn't work on the cross at his home because he didn't want his mother to know what he was doing. He couldn't claim or feign devoutness as his reason for making the cross. His mother knew he would never be driven to such an extreme by his devoutness. She would immediately guess his reasons if she knew about the cross and would forbid him to complete it.

So, Hesus had dragged the large beams out to the edge of the rice fields near Nene's home and worked there. Under the intense sun and the eyes of the broken-backed farmers in the rice paddies, Hesus began sanding all the rough spots out of the wood.

Every day that week, Nene had walked by the nearly bare patch of ground where a couple of goats were grazing and where Hesus worked on his cross. Every day, twice a day, she brought food to her parents in the field. Every time she had passed Hesus she had made a show of ignoring him. But, on the fourth day, Nene noticed the raw, pink blisters on his hands and the bright, shiny sunburn on his back and took pity on him. She had led him to her home and let him work in the cool shade of the chicken coop under her house.

"Your boyfriend is crazy," her father had observed when he came home and found Hesus working under the house.

"Yes," Nene had agreed.

"Go send him home now, so we can have some peace and quiet. Besides, he disturbs the chickens."

Hesus worked under the house for two more days. On this, the sixth day, he had to finish the cross. He drove the last few nails in under the beady, accusing eyes of the chickens. He sat against one of the slender beams that kept the house tenuously rooted to the earth and wiped the sweat from his forehead. Nene looked over the top of her comic at him.

"Are you finished?"

"Not yet. I want to oil it. Do you have any oil?"

"You didn't buy any?" Nene asked sarcastically.

"No." Hesus seemed not to notice her mocking tone. Nene gave an exaggerated sigh and climbed up the rickety, bamboo stairs into her house. She returned with a small bottle of baby oil and a large can of 'Baguio Cooking Oil.' She dropped them in front of Hesus hoping they would make at least a dull thud. There was hardly any noise. She returned to her corner and started angrily reading one of her many gossip magazines.

"You could help."

"I think it's crazy," Nene shot back without looking up from her magazine.

Hesus poured the thick, golden cooking oil, which smelled vaguely of chicken fat and old meals, into his cupped hand. Oil slid through his fingers onto the wood and the dirt floor. He smeared oil on all the surfaces of the cross, kneading and caressing the wood until it glowed with a reddish-brown light.

Nene laid her magazine down. "It is beautiful," she

finally admitted. "And just in time too. The crucifixion is tomorrow."

Hesus smiled contentedly. Nene walked over and sat beside him. She laid a hand on his back and felt the blisters and heat of his sunburn. "You're so pale you burn easily."

"My father's skin," Hesus said. Nene peeled large pieces of the loose, nearly-transparent skin off his back. It was pale. Pale and so dry it fell apart in her hand. The skin of his father.

Hesus' father was an American who had come through the barrio years ago. "The television man" they had called him whenever they talked about him. No one knew his name, except (so they assumed) Hesus' mother, or, if they had once known it, they had long ago forgotten it. Nene, like the other townspeople, often wondered which, if any, of the many men she saw on the television in Mayor Balimbing's coffee shop was Hesus' father. She took it for granted that Hesus wondered too although he never did so aloud.

Hesus' father was one of the men in the first television crew to visit the town. So the story went, they drove into town on a hot, rainy day, unusual and unwelcome weather for April. It was the day before the annual fiesta and the townspeople worried it would not clear up enough for them to celebrate the next day.

But the television men, along with an elegantly dressed Filipino man who turned out to be from the Bureau of Tourism, ran about in the rain and muck and mud shouting back and forth to each other and conferring with the astounded and very confused mayor. That evening the rain stopped and everyone slept fitfully in the still and heavy darkness. In the morning a few last-minute changes were made to the procession route and the television men sent back to America the first live footage of a bloody religious celebration featuring penitents flogging themselves and reenacting the crucifixion of Jesus.

The town was never the same after that. The people were

the same people who had lived there for generations, but the town changed. Every year in anticipation of the third week in April, in the streets along the new procession route, potholes were filled and houses repaired and painted. A small but profitable religious souvenir industry cropped up.

Hesus was born prematurely on the morning of December 24, a day before the original Jesus, but his mother gave him the name anyway. Instead of being an outcast, he was welcomed as the son of the unknown television man who had made the town famous.

Now, sixteen years later, Hesus was trying to find his father. Over the past week, most of the town had seen Hesus working or heard about what he was doing. They guessed he was trying to bring his father back, but, having no proof, were reluctant to approach his mother with their information.

"Even if you get on television, how will your father know it's you?" Nene asked as she rubbed oil into Hesus' back.

"I look like him. My mother tells me so." Hesus stared at the open blisters on his hands. Nene gently took one of his hands and began applying oil to it. "And I know my family name."

Nene's hands remained suspended a few inches over his. "It's been our secret. My name is Smith." Nene wanted to cry but instead took his hand up again and lay kisses on his blisters.

"Ay, Hesus." Her kisses pressed deeper into his flesh. Their skin soaked in the damp, dust-scented air as they lay heavily on the dirt floor. They awoke an hour later to the clucking of the chickens and the sharp pecks of the chickens' beaks against their thighs.

The chickens started laying eggs again the next morning. Nene carefully laid all but two of the eggs in her wicker basket. They always let a few of the eggs hatch in order to replace the chickens that died or were eaten by the family. She hesitated a moment then put two more eggs back.

Hesus was waiting for her outside the chicken coop. "You're early," she said.

"I didn't want to be late," Hesus replied.

"You may have a long wait."

"I don't mind." He smiled. "I've been waiting a long time already."

"Your cross is inside." Nene nodded towards the door of the chicken coop. "Will you be able to carry it into town by yourself?"

"If I have to. But I'll see if I can catch a ride on a jeepney." Hesus absently picked at a blister on his hand. "Will you be there?" He spoke quietly, but Nene heard the pleading in his voice.

"Of course," Nene replied calmly. Hesus relaxed and dropped his hands back to his side. "My mother is waiting for me." Nene raised the basket of eggs to make her point. "I have to help with breakfast."

"I'll see you at the procession then."

"Yes."

Nene climbed up the rickety ladder into her home. She heard Hesus huffing and the chickens clucking under the house as she fried the rice and eggs for breakfast. Her family heard the noise too, but they knew what it was and so ignored it. Nene watched him trudge slowly from the house and along the road into town carrying the cross on his back. She watched him so intently she nearly burned the eggs.

When Nene's family got to town, a small crowd was already gathered along the procession route even though it was still an hour till the procession started. The streets were beginning to fill with the usual fiesta trash: bright red and yellow paper tissue, crushed plastic cups, popsicle sticks, corn cobs, barbeque sticks, and occasional religious trinkets (mostly crucifixes) dropped by tourists.

Nene had left her family by one of the many large tour buses parked in front of Mayor Balimbing's coffee shop. Buses always stopped there. It was the largest, cleanest coffee shop in town and Mayor Balimbing had an exclusive and lucrative agreement with the bus company. At this time of year his coffee shop was a popular gathering spot not just for tourists, but also for town residents who came to see the strangers invading their town.

The tourists were beginning to flow out and along the main street, mingling with the townspeople. Nene weaved through a group of smartly-dressed, dark-haired, pale-skinned men and women speaking Japanese. They were mostly young and pale as the rice Nene's parents nurtured, bent over in the fields all day.

Nene continued to wander through the crowd, picking her way carefully among the trash and the people. She looked intently at the faces she passed, searching for some of her girlfriends whom she hadn't seen since the summer began.

Few of the faces she passed were familiar. It is an uneasy feeling, she thought, to walk through your own town and feel like a stranger. She passed a group of Americans, pink and blistered like Hesus from the sun, speaking their familiar and intimidating language. Their voices tapped at her head like those of the teachers in the school where Nene and the other students were required to learn English. Nene spoke English well but had the same uneasy feeling toward it that she had toward being a stranger in her own town.

Nene inched further up the street, stopping briefly to greet Aling Rosa through the one window of her sari-sari store. Aling Rosa complained about the rude tourists but smiled happily as she did so. Of course the tourists were rude but they bought everything she had. Nene continued down the street.

She tripped on some cords plugged into a large, dull gray generator squatting in the gutter among discarded wrappers and broken bottles. A large, hairy, pink hand grabbed her by the arm and stopped her fall.

43

"Watch it, girl," the large man behind the hand said, as he hauled her up. "You could lose us some valuable footage."

Nene was overwhelmed by his presence. "Excuse me," she replied meekly. He ignored her. Still with a firm grip on her arm he turned to yell behind him.

"Ey Joe!" He paused. "Velasco!" A very dark, slightly plump Filipino man came stumbling out of the crowd.

"Ya boss?"

"Get some of the boys to watch the generator will you?" The large man gestured at Nene with his free hand. "This girl nearly took out power to some of our equipment. We'd be in a hell of a fix if that happened while we were transmitting to Manila."

Joe nodded. "Okay boss. Will do." And he disappeared into the crowd again. Through the few gaps in the crowd, Nene now saw the cameras and the other unidentifiable equipment positioned just on the other side of the barricades. The large man noticed that he was still gripping her arm and hastily dropped it as if it were a dead animal.

Nene rubbed at the fat, red marks his fingers had left just below the line of her shirt sleeve. "Hope I didn't hurt you," he mumbled. Nene shook her head. Joe returned with two "boys." They were two young men who looked overeager and excited about the work they were doing with the television crew. The large man, "boss" they all called him, posted one on either side of the generator.

"Girl, could you do me a favor?" The boss didn't wait for her answer. "Go over to one of the stores nearby and buy us some sodas." He turned to Joe. "How many do we need?"

"Six, ... No seven."

"Make it ten." He fumbled in his pocket. "Here's twenty pesos." Nene plucked the wadded-up bill from his large, sweaty palm. "We'll be over there." He pointed toward the cameras and swatted her on the behind to get her going.

Nene jumped in embarrassment. She walked hurriedly

44

down the street, trying to get as far from him as possible and hoping that no one she knew had noticed his crude behavior. At Aling Rosa's sari-sari stores she bought five Cokes and five Sprites. Aling Rosa placed the bottles of soda in an empty, wooden crate so Nene could carry them all.

Nene first offered sodas to the two "boys" guarding the generator. They shyly accepted. Then she had to make her way through the crowd that always gathered around the television crew hoping to be part of the glamorous world they represented. Nene had always found television glamorous too, but now she felt trapped by the large television man who loomed before her.

Nene offered him a soda and tried to return his change. He waved her away in irritation and indicated that she should keep the change. After distributing all the drinks she could, she stood forlornly in the midst of the cables and equipment and men with the leftover sodas. The edges of the wooden crate were digging into her fingers.

"Wait here," the large boss, the television man, said. "I may need you later."

Nene nodded and shifted the crate in her hands. She hoped the procession would be over quickly so she could leave. From down the street, she heard the wailing of the penitents approaching. As they drew nearer, she could hear the sharp hiss and slap of the whips as the men flailed them against their flesh.

Their wails crashed against the crowd and dissipated among the faces. The smell of sweat and dirt and blood preceded them. Nene saw the whips flash through the air and slash through the men's already mortified flesh. She felt the heat from their bodies as they passed by her.

Blood sprayed from the whips and from the men's bare and torn backs. A drop landed on the corner of Nene's lips. She licked it. It was bitter and tasted of leather and sweat.

The penitents passed, leaving their blood on the streets.

They were followed by seven men carrying seven crosses. Nene saw Hesus. He was in front of the group. He must have fought for that position.

When they reached the television cameras, the men stopped and laid their crosses on the ground. A small group of men at the end of the procession rushed up to the crosses with hammers and nails. Nene watched as a young man with a faint mustache above his lip and long, slim fingers drove a nail through Hesus' right hand.

The young man looked frightened and his hands seemed unsteady. Hesus closed his eyes and bit his bottom lip. His lip started bleeding, but he continued to bite down on it. Finally, the young man raised the cross and Hesus hung before the crowd.

Blood trickled from his lip and his tongue hung limply from his mouth. The sweat shone on his limbs, which appeared to be relaxed. Even his fingers drooped. All that moved were his eyes, which twitched frantically back and forth scanning the crowd but seeing nothing.

Slowly, the other crosses around him were raised. They swayed before the crowd, their human burdens hanging like trophies. Somewhere behind Nene someone retched. It stank. Everything around her stank. The air was too thick with blood and bile.

Hesus' cross was lowered to the ground. The television cameras crowded around him focusing on his frantic eyes, his mouth flecked with blood and saliva. He mumbled softly. Nene thought she heard "Smith." Then they pried the nails out and blood poured from the holes. Hesus fainted.

The television man supervised the cameramen as they focused on the holes and the blood. Nene felt blood on her right hand and dropped the wooden crate. A long, jagged piece of wood on the edge of the crate had cut her palm and left a splinter in it. She pulled the splinter out and pressed her hand against her jeans to stop the bleeding.

Nene looked back at Hesus and saw that his hands were covered in blood. A thin sheen of red liquid floated in his palms and trickled onto the damp, littered street. He shouldn't be bleeding so much. It should have slowed by now, Nene realized. The young man who had nailed Hesus to the cross realized it too and watched in horror as the blood continued to flow profusely.

The young man removed his shirt and pressed down hard on one of Hesus' hands. The shirt was soon stained and heavy with blood. Another man came to help him. Soon a small group of men was clustered around Hesus. They spoke hurriedly and frantically to each other but didn't seem to be listening. They seemed to speak more for reassurance than out of necessity.

Each one took his turn placing his head against Hesus' chest. Nene took in their worried looks and Hesus' limp body draining onto the street. He's dead, she thought.

A woman began to cry and pray. "Lamb of God ...." Nene was knocked to the ground by an American woman who had fainted. Nene sat in the road among the dirt and paper wrappers and discarded bits of food. She reached for the wooden crate and pulled herself to it. With her hands gripping the crate tightly, Nene vomited into it.

Her breath came in heaves. She had to force herself to breathe in. The wound on her hand reopened and she could feel the blood oozing out onto the crate. She started screaming.

On and on the screams shook her body. Nene realized in horror that she couldn't stop. "Hesus! Hesus! Hesus!" She saw feet running around her and heard other voices getting louder and more hysterical. The familiar large, pink hand of the television man appeared, grabbed her by the arm, and dragged her to her feet. He pulled her through the crowd, colliding with tourists, vendors, and stray cats and dogs. Nene stumbled along after him. The noise converged around them. Individual screams and cries were lost in the large, pulsing sound that was the crowd. Nene took several deep, painful breaths as she ran and was finally able to stop screaming. But now she could smell and taste the stench in her mouth.

It seemed that they had been running blindly for so long that Nene was surprised to find they were only at the small hotel behind Mayor Balimbing's coffee shop. The television man dragged her through the cramped, anemically-lit lobby, and down a short corridor to the end of the hall. He stopped in front of a door and searched in his pockets for his keys. Nene whimpered.

He held the door open and scowled at her as she entered. "Well, you certainly added drama to our coverage. You and your boyfriend." The television man sighed. "I assume that was him on the cross." He flicked a couple of light switches until he finally found one that worked. A pale, yellow light trembled above a lopsided couch, a dented coffee table, and a low bed with a large depression in the center.

The room was surprisingly neat. The bed was made. There was no trash lying about. Everything appeared to be in its place. It was the television man's room and Nene, the stranger, felt very uneasy.

"I doubt they'll be able to use the audio on that. The commentary was damn near drowned out by your screaming and the rest of the noise." He flicked the bathroom light on. "What a way to get on television." Nene heard him running some water in the sink. "Hesus. God." He came out and looked at Nene, who was crying by the coffee table. "Listen, I'm sorry about what happened. I mean, it's terrible that your boyfriend ...." He paused uneasily. His fingers fidgeted with the towel he held. "Um, why don't you wash up? Here's a towel and there's some soap in there." He indicated the bathroom. Nene took the towel.

The water as still running in the sink although it was only a little more than a trickle. Nene tried the shower, but it wasn't working, so she stoppered up the sink and soaked her head in the water until she had to come up for air. The soap stung her eyes and the mouthwash she found in the medicine cabinet stung her mouth and throat. Nene was glad for the pain, like the sharp burning of a raw wound. It felt right that she should hurt.

When she emerged from the bathroom, the television man was fumbling with the dial of his small transistor radio. There was too much static though and he turned it off impatiently. "Feel better?" He asked. Nene nodded.

"Listen ... where do you live?" He shifted uneasily on the sofa. "I mean, I can't let you stay here ..... Your parents must be looking for you." He fiddled with the tuner on the dead radio. "I could call a jeepney for you and have the driver take you home."

Nene sat on the edge of the bed and started crying again. The man became flustered. "Don't cry ... please."

He sat beside her and lay a thick arm around her shoulders. Nene continued to shudder and cry uncontrollably. Hesitantly, he began to stroke her hair. She dropped her head on his chest and continued crying. "Shhhh.... Oh God," the television man sighed as he stroked her hair.

Nene wrapped her thin arms around him and kissed his chest as she cried. He recoiled at first but didn't push her away. Instead he wrapped his arms around her and held her as they slid down into the depression in the center of the bed.

Nene imagined she was in the chicken coop under her house with Hesus. The damp ground was under them and the fuzzy outlines of the dirty, white chickens surrounded them.

An American Romance

She met him when he came in to exchange money at the small Filipino handicrafts store where she worked. It wasn't payday she knew, so she was surprised when he gave her fifty dollars. Most sailors didn't have that much money two days before payday. She gave him seven hundred pesos.

He looked surprised. "Seven hundred?" She nodded.

He was new. Probably just come from Diego Garcia. That was why he had so much money. No place to spend it there.

"Thanks," he said and gave her a big grin. His wide, black hands scooped up the bills. "They said this place was cheap, but I didn't think it would be this cheap." He put the money in his wallet. He tapped the wallet against the counter and seemed to be thinking as he glanced around the store. Finally, he looked back at her. "What's your name?"

She was surprised and he must have mistaken her surprise for misunderstanding because he repeated himself. "Your name?" he exaggerated his words and pointed at her. She could feel a tingling on her neck, just above the collarbone, where his finger was pointed.

"Evelyn," she whispered shyly.

"Hi Evelyn!" He broke into another big smile that showed his teeth, a startling, bright white against his dark face. "I'm Macarthur!" He held out his right hand. She reached over the counter and offered her hand, which he shook with great enthusiasm. He didn't release her hand right away, so she gently withdrew it.

51

"So, um, what time do you get off work?" He leaned against the counter. She wished another customer would come along, but it was still early in the afternoon.

"Seven o'clock," she whispered again. He was making her nervous.

"Well maybe we could go have a drink."

"No." She shook her head.

"No?"

"No." She stared at the counter top.

"Are you sure?" he insisted.

"No."

"No? Then you're not sure." She looked at him in confusion. He smiled as if to put her at ease. "You said no, you're not sure, so maybe you do want to go and have a drink with me." She realized he was teasing her.

"No." She shook her head emphatically. "No, I do not want to drink with you."

Another customer, a middle-aged Filipino man, walked down the stairs from the street and headed toward her counter. The young sailor saw him.

"All right." He pushed himself away from the counter and stood up straight. "But, maybe you'll be thirsty at seven." He tucked his wallet into his back pocket and turned to leave.

"You shouldn't put your money there," she called after him. "Someone might take it."

He drew the wallet from his back pocket and placed it in one of the pockets in his jacket. "Thanks." He winked at her and waved goodbye. She gave him a weak smile. "See you at seven," he called and climbed up the stairs to the street.

The middle-aged Filipino man pulled a few carefully folded dollar bills out of a small coin purse he held in his hand. She counted five dollars and gave him seventy pesos. He slowly folded the bills, placed them in the coin purse and dropped the coin purse into a small paper bag he was carrying.

She watched him as he walked up the stairs. He was short

and bony, neatly dressed in a faded red t-shirt and jeans with his hair slicked back. He reminded her of her father who was a yardman. The man walking up the stairs probably was a yardman too, one of those who trimmed hedges and cut grass for those who lived on the military base.

The man disappeared up the stairs and out the door. She saw his feet, in blue and white tennis shoes, walk along the long strip of window facing the street. She sat down on her stool behind the counter and started to look through a magazine for the second time, reading the articles that she had ignored the first time around. The air conditioning unit shuddered noisily behind her and the condensation dripped into the large, powdered milk can on the floor.

A few minutes before five a couple of men walked into the store. Before she was finished with them, a woman lined up behind them to get her money changed. After the woman left, the owner of the store came in to check on business and take most of the dollars to the bank. She left Evelyn with more pesos and some dollars.

The rest of the evening a fairly steady flow of customers, workers from the base, and sailors came into the store to exchange their dollars. A few of the sailors looked at the baskets, the carved wooden figures, the wall hangings, the purses, the small collection of silver jewelry behind the glass counter where Evelyn sat. No one bought anything, but a few of them seemed to be considering the goods carefully, perhaps making a mental note to come back and buy souvenirs before they left. The owner returned and disappeared into her office.

Evelyn saw Macarthur walk in a few minutes before seven. He wandered among the shelves of handicrafts and she pretended not to see him while she helped the last few customers. The customers left, and Evelyn busied herself with dusting the counter top and polishing the silver jewelry displayed beneath it.

The owner walked out of her office a few minutes after seven. She finished eating the banana she had in her hand, brushed her hands on her skirt and adjusted her glasses on her nose. Then she noticed Macarthur standing by the small wooden warrior statue in the back of the store.

"We're closed, sir!" the owner called out.

"I know." He walked toward the counter. "I'm waiting for Evelyn."

He gave the owner his big, startling grin. She was unmoved and looked skeptically at him through the small glasses perched on her nose. She turned to Evelyn, her lips pressed together into a thin line, which Evelyn knew was a sign of displeasure.

"I .... I'm sorry, ma'am," Evelyn said, her voice wavering. "I don't want him to."

The owner pulled her glasses off and gave a big sigh. She let the glasses drop and swing slightly from the chain around her neck. "He has to leave. I can't finish business while he is in the store."

Evelyn turned to Macarthur. He had already heard the owner and was backing out towards the street.

"It's all right. I'll wait for you outside."

He ran up the stairs two at a time. The owner watched until he had walked out onto the street, then she walked across the store and up the stairs to lock the door. Evelyn could see Macarthur's feet in his high-top white and black sneakers standing by the door.

She fidgeted behind the counter, wishing that she could begin counting the money so she would have something to do but knowing she couldn't until the owner returned. The owner didn't like to have anyone count the money unless she was there to watch. Evelyn didn't think this made much sense since the owner did leave her alone with the money during the day.

The owner opened the cash register and counted out the

money while Evelyn wrote the amounts down on a sheet of paper. They bundled the bills together, put the coins into the paper rolls and placed everything in a dirty, brown burlap bag with "Bank of the Philippine Islands" in faded lettering on it. The owner locked her office door while Evelyn locked the jewelry case. Then they walked up the stairs together. Evelyn noticed that the white and black high-top sneakers were still waiting by the door.

"Maybe you can have your boyfriend walk me to my car," the owner said to Evelyn as they slowly climbed the stairs. "Joey couldn't come with me today. His father needed him to help move some furniture." She breathed heavily as she climbed towards the door.

"Ma'am, he's not my boyfriend," Evelyn protested. "I don't know him."

"Well ...." The owner paused to unlock the door. She held it open for Evelyn and they walked out into a gentle rain. Macarthur was leaning against the glass window of the shop above the handicraft store in an attempt to keep out of the rain. The owner glanced at him. "He looks nice enough. Maybe he can walk me to the car anyway." She locked the door. "It's just around the corner."

Evelyn didn't reply. She was trying to focus all of her attention on her umbrella, which wouldn't open. She finally gave up in frustration and faced Macarthur. "Ah ... my boss, she needs help to walk to her car, to guard the money." Evelyn indicated the small, brown burlap bag in her owner's arms.

"Sure!" he agreed and held out his hands to receive the bag.

"I can carry it," the owner said. She handed her account ledger and books to Evelyn to carry, then led the way down the street. They tried to stay under the awnings on the front of the stores in order to keep dry. They passed the record store, the department store, and a little doughnut shop on the corner. Just around the corner was the owner's old, light blue car.

She got into the driver's side and threw the money bag into the front seat beside her. Evelyn used her body to shield the account ledger and the books from the rain as she passed them through the front window. The owner leaned across the passenger seat towards them.

"Thank you Mr. ...?" she called through the open window.

"Macarthur," he replied. "Macarthur Moreaux." He stood with his hands in his jacket pockets. Rain trickled from the top of his head down the rest of his body.

"Thank you, Mr. Moreaux ... Macarthur. Please come by the store anytime."

"Oh, I will," he eagerly agreed.

He and Evelyn stepped back under the awning and waited for the owner to drive off. Her car belched a puff of gray smoke as soon as the engine started. A light, steady wisp of smoke streamed from the exhaust pipe. As soon as the road was clear, she pulled a U-turn from her parking space and puffed down the street.

Macarthur turned to Evelyn. "Where would you like to go?"

"I have to go home."

"Can't we go have a drink for just a little while?"

"My family is waiting for me."

"Well, maybe we could just have a doughnut or something from that store." He pointed to the little doughnut shop on the corner.

"No." Evelyn started backing away towards the main street. "I have to be home for dinner."

Macarthur followed her. "I'll walk you back to the corner then."

They walked quickly and silently in single file under the storefront awnings. At the corner Evelyn squeezed into the last available bit of seating room on a jeepney. She was wedged into the back corner beside an old woman with a huge grocery bag full of empty soda bottles.

The jeepney moved forward slowly in the long line of jeepneys along the curb. Macarthur waved goodbye. His face was shiny from the rain and little raindrops glittered like a cap on his tight, curly hair.

The jeepney reached the front of the line and suddenly sped up. The old lady's bottles clanked against one another. Evelyn turned back to wave goodbye to Macarthur, but he was already walking down the street toward the clubs.

Evelyn didn't see Macarthur the next day or the day after that. She was a little disappointed the first day because she had expected him to return. On the second day she was relieved that he didn't show up. She didn't know what she would say to him.

Just before closing on the third day after their meeting, Evelyn saw the familiar white and black high-top sneakers standing by the glass outside the door. She was agitated and made mistakes on the sheet of paper that she wrote the day's totals on. As she walked up the stairs, Evelyn tried to stay very close to the owner and the owner's son, Joey, so that maybe Macarthur wouldn't notice her among them.

Macarthur was talking to two other sailors when they walked out of the store. Evelyn thought that maybe he wouldn't see her, but he looked up as she passed by. The owner recognized him and smiled.

"Hello, Macarthur."

"Hello, ma'am," he replied politely and bowed slightly toward her. "Hi Evelyn." The owner and her son walked down the street to their car.

"Hi, Macarthur," Evelyn said quietly.

"Do you have to be home early tonight?"

"Yes." She looked down at the sidewalk.

"You don't have time for a drink or anything?"

"No. I have to go home."

"Well ...." He ran a hand across his hair.

"Come on Macarthur." His two friends started backing down the street. "Come on! Let's go!" They were still walking backwards and yelling at him as they walked. "Aaahh. Forget him," the short, black sailor said and they both turned their backs on Macarthur.

He watched them walk down the street then turned back to Evelyn. "Are you sure you wouldn't like to come along?" He hesitated for a moment. "We don't have to stay with them. They're kind of rowdy. Um, ... I know you probably don't drink, so we could just go have a Coke or Seven-Up or whatever."

"No, I ..." Evelyn began.

"Maaaac!" the taller, white sailor called out. He was walking back toward them. "Come on!" He stopped just across the street. "You're just wasting your time, man."

"Yeah, man!" the other sailor shouted from further away. "She's not like that. There's lots of girls in this city!" He paused to catch his breath. "And they ain't so hard to get as that!"

Macarthur waved angrily at them to go away. The one closest flung his hands up in the air in disgust and they both left. "Hey, don't listen to them," he said to Evelyn, who was standing quietly with her head down. "They're just ...." He grimaced to show what he thought of them. "I'm sorry about what they said."

"I have to go," Evelyn almost whispered.

"Yeah. Yeah. Okay, I understand." Macarthur had his hands in his pockets and was bouncing lightly on his feet, shifting around in his white and black shoes. "Hey, forget about them, okay?"

Evelyn nodded. "Goodbye," she said.

"Goodbye."

She found an almost-full jeepney near the front of the line

and squeezed in. A few moments later it sped off around the corner. Macarthur stood in front of the store with his hands in his pockets watching her jeepney leave.

She didn't see him for almost a week; he didn't stop by the store or wait outside the door, and she was sure that he had decided to leave her alone. In fact, the next time they met was an accident or at least seemed an accident. It was raining hard when Evelyn walked out of the store, so she ran to the doughnut shop on the corner to wait for a jeepney. For some reason, there weren't many jeepneys by the curb at that time and the few that were there were full.

It wasn't until she was inside the shop that she saw Macarthur. He was sitting at one of the two small tables in the very small shop carefully eating a gooey, chocolate-covered doughnut. She couldn't just ignore him, so she smiled and he raised his hand in greeting while he swallowed.

"Hello."

"Hello," he said through the napkin with which he was wiping his mouth. "How are you doing?"

"I'm fine."

"Have a seat." He gestured to the only other chair at his table. She sat down, perched on the edge of the chair. "Raining pretty hard out there."

"Yes."

"You on your way home?"

Evelyn nodded.

"You want a doughnut while you wait?"

"No."

"You're gonna be here a while."

"A jeepney will go by soon."

"You gonna take a jeepney in this rain?"

"Yes."

"Listen, why don't I take you home?" He stood up and threw his napkin into the trashcan as if shooting a basketball. "I got a car now and it's just down the street."

"No, I can wait."

"I don't mind, really. And it's not as if we're strangers or anything."

"No."

"Well, you could be waiting awhile because they got some kind of construction going on up the street and the jeepneys are having trouble getting through." He sat back down in his chair and smiled at her smugly. "I know you have to be home on time."

Evelyn hesitated to accept the offer. She peered through the rain-splattered glass out into the street. There were no jeepneys coming and the last few lined up against the curb had left. She stared down at her hands in her lap and looked back up at Macarthur. He was looking out the window, but he turned slightly and looked at her out of the corner of his eyes.

Evelyn sighed. "It's my father's birthday," she confessed.

"Then you'd better get home on time." He stood up and stretched his arms and bounced on his feet. "Where do you live?"

"West Bajac Bajac." She stood up too.

"Where's that?"

"Toward the mountains, near Rizal Triangle."

He thought over her directions for a moment. "Okay ... Okay, I can find it."

"Are you sure? You won't get lost on the way back?"

"No. I'm good at finding my way around."

"Okay."

"You ready to go?" He started for the door.

"Yes." She followed him.

"Oh! Wait a minute." He headed back to the counter. "Let's get some doughnuts for your father." He rapped on the counter to attract the attention of the counterperson in the back of the shop. "Your Dad like doughnuts?"

"Oh, no. You don't have to," she pleaded, embarrassed.

"It's okay. I don't mind."

"Please don't. It's not necessary," Evelyn begged. She didn't want to have to explain the doughnuts when she got home.

"What kind does he like?" Macarthur asked. The young girl who came out of the back of the store looked bored.

"I don't know." Evelyn felt flustered. "I don't know if he has ever eaten doughnuts."

"Never had a doughnut?" Macarthur pretended shock.

"I don't know. I don't think ...." Evelyn trailed off miserably.

"Well, let's get him one of each kind then." Macarthur turned to the girl behind the counter. "One chocolate, one plain ... the powdered sugar kind, um, the jelly doughnut ...."

Evelyn listened unhappily as Macarthur picked out a dozen doughnuts. The girl put them in a large pink box with a cartoon picture of a doughnut man on the top. Macarthur put his jacket over the box so that the doughnuts wouldn't get wet when they walked out into the rain.

Macarthur's car was parked at the end of the street where the Catholic school was. They didn't have any umbrellas and there were no awnings along the street, so they ran down the sidewalk as fast as possible trying not to get too wet. Macarthur jumped over a muddy puddle on the sidewalk. Evelyn ran around but ended up getting drenched under a drainage pipe that was running water off the roof of the school.

They both got into the car and Macarthur handed her the doughnuts, which smelled nauseatingly sweet in the closed, muggy space. The engine idled loudly. Evelyn felt sticky and uncomfortable and upset that she was dripping all over the car seat and floor. The box of doughnuts sat like a lump on her lap.

"Which way?" Macarthur asked.

Evelyn began to give him directions, and they drove carefully down the rainy, potholed street. She thought the easiest route would be to go through the main streets as much as possible. They would have to get on the side streets eventually, but as long as he drove most of the way on the main streets maybe he wouldn't get lost on the way back. Macarthur left he main street only for a short, twisting detour around the construction. They saw a lot of jeepneys going in the opposite direction stuck in the mud in the middle of the main detour route.

They drove along past the many neon nightclubs where her eyes were bombarded by the lights and the colorful people lurking just inside the doorways. Still, all Evelyn could hear was the dull, steady knocking of the rain against the car. They drove further down, past the smaller and less colorful clubs until the streets were lit only by streetlights and the light that spilled out from inside shops.

Evelyn finally directed Macarthur to turn off the main road and they snaked down a little side street, avoiding the jeepneys and tricycles parked at random along both sides. Evelyn saw some of the people lounging inside the vehicles turn to look as she and Macarthur drove by, and she wondered if they could see her. They turned down another darker and more deteriorated side street. The car rattled and shook as they drove down narrow side street after narrow side street.

"You live way out here," Macarthur said more as a comment than a question.

"Around this corner," Evelyn replied.

"Which way?"

"Right." Macarthur turned right.

"That house." Evelyn pointed at an old, wooden, two-story house across the street. It looked dark green in the weak light from the streetlamp, but it was more of a light, pastel green, a popular color because it was readily available and cheap. Macarthur stopped the car, rolled down his window and looked at it. A dog barked inside the rust-colored gate.

Light came through the curtains on the bottom floor and

the faint sounds of a television, laughter, and voices reached the car. Rain spilled in a torrent from the drainpipe on the roof down onto the concrete front "yard" of the house. Another dog joined the first one at the gate and they barked and shivered in the rain. The lone woman in the sari-sari store at the corner set down her magazine to stare at the car sitting in the rain.

"You live here?" Macarthur said incredulously.

"Yes," Evelyn replied a bit forcefully.

Macarthur didn't seem to notice that he had insulted her. "God, this is run down." He continued to stare at the house. "So you live here." He glanced around the neighborhood.

"We live on the bottom floor," Evelyn explained.

"Not on the top floor?"

"No. The bottom floor only."

"Just the bottom floor? Your whole family lives on the bottom floor? How many of you are there?"

Evelyn didn't say anything.

Macarthur continued to look around the neighborhood. "You know ...." He paused as he glanced from house to house. "You should come on the base with me sometime. I could show you around ...." He sat back in his seat. "We could even drive through the housing area and you could see some of the houses. It's nothing like the States, but it ain't like this either." He gestured toward the street outside the car. "Man, how can you live here?" Macarthur turned to her.

"I live here," Evelyn replied quietly.

"It's just ...." He made a face. "You ever seen what people live in in the States?"

"On television." Evelyn sat hunched in her seat.

"So how can you live here?"

Evelyn remained silent, trying to keep herself from screaming at Macarthur. Her throat felt sore and tense. She sat up quickly and nearly knocked the doughnuts off her lap.

"Do you like it?" Macarthur persisted, as if challenging her.

Evelyn didn't know what to say and was afraid to say anything for fear of crying in front of him. She fumbled with the door handle of the car and opened the door. Rain came in as she stepped out with the doughnuts.

"Evelyn!" Macarthur reached for her but she was already out of the car. "Evelyn!" he yelled through his window.

Evelyn waded through the muddy water swirling in the street, some of it backed up from the garbage-filled canals. The dogs barked in recognition of her and she walked toward them, ignoring the rain and Macarthur. Tears and rain ran down her face.

"Evelyn!" he yelled but didn't attempt to get out of the car.

She reached the gate and opened it. The dogs jumped up at her, nosing her pants and shoes and the box of doughnuts. The gate closed with a loud clang on Macarthur sitting silently in his car.

Evelyn dropped the doughnut box into the stream of water that flowed across the concrete yard and out into the street. She walked into her house. The dogs tipped the box over, grabbed a soggy doughnut each in their jaws and ran off under the eaves of the house to eat them.

In the Neon City by the River

There was no breeze at all in the air and the river stank. Teresa looked down at the black water as they walked over the bridge. It was a muddy, thick black that looked like it could suck her in. Rusty pipes stuck out of the rock-and-concrete walls that rose up on either side of the river. At certain hours of the day, sewage from the city spilled out of these pipes. Teresa had never actually seen this happen, but she saw the floating debris, the discolored water and smelled the stench. She imagined the sewage spilled out at night when nobody was watching.

Four young boys were swimming in the river amid the human wastes of the city. They yelled at the sailors passing by.

"Ey Joe! Gimme peso? Ey Joe!"

Two sailors dressed up for a night out stopped and stared over the railing at the boys.

"How can they swim in that shit?"

"Shit, I don't know."

"You got a peso?" The taller of the two asked his friend. "Whatcha do for a peso, boy?"

Teresa and her friends passed them by. Her friends were talking and laughing as they walked along. Teresa stared blankly at the backs of the Filipino workers who were only now getting off work. Cocky young sailors and marines eager for a night on the town weaved quickly in and out of the crowd.

A young girl and an older woman at the end of the bridge caught Teresa's eye. They were arguing. People walking off the bridge made a wide circle around them to avoid getting involved. The woman made sharp motions with her hands to accentuate what she was saying. The girl pulled nervously at her short, uncombed brown hair. She had a clean, almost-innocent face—about thirteen or fourteen years old, Teresa guessed. Her long arms stuck awkwardly out of her sleeveless dress, and she pulled self-consciously on the faded skirt that she had long ago grown too tall to wear.

"Bruha!" Teresa heard as she approached the couple. "Walang utang na loob!" The girl burst into tears. The woman grabbed her by the hand and dragged her off into the city.

Once they were off the bridge and into the city, the air was hot and smelled strongly of the diesel fumes belching from the jeepneys that whizzed by. The cool, empty glare of neon washed the street and the people in gaudy reds and yellows. Greg poked her in the shoulder.

"What do you think?" he said.

"Ow!" Teresa rubbed her shoulder. "About what?"

"About what?" Karen mimicked her in a high-pitched voice. Myrna giggled.

"I'm sorry. I wasn't listening."

"Yeah. I guess not," Greg said. "About where we should go."

"I don't care. Wherever you all want to go."

Karen rolled her eyes in exasperation. "That's what we're trying to decide."

"Okay. Okay."

"So, where do you want to go?"

"Fillmore?"

"They have good daquiris at Cordon Blue," Dave suggested.

"Dave just wants to go there because one of the dancers hangs all over him," Karen said.

66

Dave was too embarrassed to reply. They walked along the sidewalk in front of the bars. Loud rock music and heavy smoke poured out of the doorways. Some shy Filipino women and some more aggressive ones hung around in front of the bars trying to attract the sailors that were cruising by. The shy ones hid in the dark doorways of the bars and just said "hi" and giggled nervously. The more aggressive women planted themselves in the middle of the sidewalk and tried to strike up a conversation as the men walked around them.

"Well, where are we going?" Greg asked again.

"I vote for Fillmore," Karen said.

"I think Jerry and them said they were going to be at Sierra tonight," Myrna suggested.

"I'd rather go to Fillmore," said Teresa.

"Yeah, me too," Dave added quickly.

They continued to walk down the sidewalk into the heart of the bars and clubs. A few of the women came up to Greg and Dave. Greg just ignored them. They made Dave nervous and although he tried to ignore them it was obvious he couldn't, so the women pestered him even more. Greg had to tell them to leave.

Karen stopped at a sidewalk stall that was selling caps and other souvenirs. "Hey, look at this." She held a cap before them. It was blue with gold braid and the Navy insignia in the center. "Ask him how much it is, Teresa."

"Magkano ba ito?"

"Forty-five pesos."

"Ang mahal naman. Twenty-five."

"Ay, hindi puede."

Teresa turned to walk away.

"O, sige." The man behind the stall called her back. "Forty."

"Twenty-five."

"Thirty."

"You want to pay thirty pesos?" Teresa asked Karen.

"Yeah. That's okay." She took thirty pesos from her purse and they walked off with the cap.

"Can we stop and change some money first?" Myrna asked.

"Yeah, I gotta change some money too," Dave said.

"Let's go to Flora's then," said Teresa. "They have good rates."

"Okay." Greg agreed and dashed out into the street.

"Greg!" Teresa called after him.

A jeepney was approaching but Greg held his hand out and it slowed down. The rest of them followed. Another jeepney was approaching quickly in the other lane, but Greg held out his hand again and the driver jammed down on his brakes. The jeepney lurched forward as it stopped and the driver scowled at them. They scurried across the street.

"Loco-loco!" A peanut vendor shook her head disapprovingly as they stepped up to the curb. She turned to a cigarette vendor standing beside her. "Loco-loco talaga ang mga batang Kano."

Teresa was embarrassed and angry. "Dammit Greg! What if they hadn't stopped?"

"Nah. They always stop for us."

They walked into Flora's, past the displays of clothes and shoes in the front, past the glass-enclosed currency exchange counter to a battered, brown counter in the very back where a middle-aged woman sat reading the evening paper. She didn't look at them until Teresa spoke.

"What's the rate today?"

"Twenty to one," she replied, setting her paper down. It was two pesos over the official rate posted on the glass-enclosed counter in the front. The woman set her elbows on the counter and leaned toward them.

"Okay," said Teresa, and they all lined up to get their money exchanged.

With the new money in their pockets, they walked out of

the store and onto the sidewalk littered with peanut shells and discarded cigarette butts. The woman selling peanuts didn't notice them. She was talking lazily with a jeepney driver who had parked by her to take a quick rest.

"Cigarette?" The cigarette vendor approached them with his tray hanging from his neck. "Pall Mall. Kool." Teresa shook her head. The others simply ignored him. "Juicy Fruit?" He tried again, this time pointing to his assortment of chewing gum.

"Oh." Myrna turned to look at the tray. "I'll have a Juicy Fruit." She bought her gum, and the man, satisfied, turned away from them and tried to interest the jeepney driver in his tray.

"Let's go!" Greg yelled. Teresa and the others turned to find him standing in the middle of the street. Brightly-colored jeepneys flashing chrome and disco lights roared up and down the street on either side of him. He smiled and waved at them. "Come on!"

"What an asshole!" Karen exclaimed.

"He's gonna get himself killed," said Dave.

"Or arrested." Teresa could see a policeman directing traffic near the bridge. "Come on. Let's go get him." No jeepneys were approaching, so they dashed into the street and tried to get their hands on Greg. He faked them out, ran along the center line, and hopped around like a boxer avoiding them. A jeepney sped by a few inches from them. Finally, they got Greg to the other side.

They stood on the curb, hot, sweaty, and panting. An audience of two small, dirty children in oversized t-shirts watched them from behind a telephone pole. Greg grinned a little crazily at his friends.

"Damn you!" Karen glared at him. "You could have gotten us killed!"

"Or arrested!" Teresa looked down the street to make sure the police officer was still at his post directing traffic.

"Hey." Greg's smile broke into a laugh. "What's the point of going out if we don't have fun?"

"That wasn't fun, Greg," Dave said seriously.

"Well then don't hang around with me, jarhead," Greg snapped back.

Dave cringed and ran his hand across his newly-cut hair.

"Let's just go to Fillmore, okay?" Myrna said softly.

They stood in tense silence. One of the street children who had been watching from behind the pole came out and touched Teresa on the arm. She shook him off. He pawed at her arm again.

"Ma'am. Peso?"

"No!" she snapped. "Come on. Let's go." She strode off down the street.

When she finally stopped, slightly out of breath, in front of the Fillmore, she saw that the others were far behind. Dave and Myrna shuffled along slowly with their heads down. Greg and Karen were obviously impatient but slowing down just for them. Teresa leaned against the wall and waited.

Now that she'd walked her anger off, she felt badly about how she'd treated the child. She hated to be approached by the street children. They often ran up to her when she walked off the bridge from the military base and flocked around her when she bought bread from the bakery on her way home. Usually she ignored them. Sometimes, overcome by guilt, she gave them money or bread. They made her feel awful.

The rest were in pretty low spirits by the time they caught up with her. They stood uncertainly in front of the door to the club. The yellow neon light blinking on and off above them made them look gray and anemic.

"Well, are we going in?" said Greg.

"Yeah, I guess so," said Karen. They half-heartedly assented and climbed the stairs.

They paused for a moment on the landing to adjust their eyes to the dim light of the club. Teresa stared at the murals surrounding her. Bright and pulsating, they seemed straight out of the psychedelic era.

There were no murals inside the club, just a lot of brightly-colored flashing lights on the dance floor and full-length mirrors interspersed along the walls. It was crowded, but they managed to find a table close to the door and the dance floor.

A waiter appeared immediately in his white dress shirt, pleated black pants and a bow tie. He was dressed better than most of the people in the club. They ordered beers and a pitcher of mojo then sat back and watched the dance floor and the people around them. It was impossible to carry on a conversation. The music was so loud Teresa could feel it beating into her.

The drinks came quickly. Teresa quickly drank two glasses of mojo. It tasted like Kool-Aid, but she started feeling dizzy while drinking the third glass. Myrna giggled at something Karen said. Myrna always giggled. Dave smiled happily and asked Teresa to dance.

They headed towards the dance floor weaving in and out of the people, mostly men, who were crowded around it. Teresa stumbled along behind Dave, who was holding her hand. She bumped into a lot of the men. They were too intent on watching the bikini-clad women gyrating on the platforms around the dance floor to care about her.

The dance floor was crowded and they could barely move. Still, Teresa felt better. It felt good to be dancing. A large women bumped into Teresa, causing her to fall into Dave. Dave caught her and laughed and they kept on dancing until they were too tired to dance anymore.

They returned to their table tired and laughing. Someone had ordered two more pitchers of mojo and Teresa helped herself to some. She glanced around at the men in the club. Some good-looking guys tonight, she thought. She wouldn't mind dancing with some of them. She could easily leave if they got to be too aggressive. That was why she always went out with a group.

One of the roaming photographers approached their table. He pointed to his camera and shouted. They couldn't understand much of what he said. It was garbled by the loud music. But they knew what he wanted and looked at each other questioningly. Heads nodded around the table. They grouped around Myrna and adjusted their clothing, fixed their hair. They smiled. The photographer took their picture and promised to be back in fifteen minutes.

Greg and Myrna got up to dance. Karen slid into the seat beside Teresa and leaned close to her ear.

"You wanna go to the bathroom?"

"What?"

"The bathroom." Karen pointed to the back of the club. Teresa nodded and got up. They left Dave alone and looking forlorn at the large table.

The bright, fluorescent light in the bathroom was a sudden shock after the artificial twilight of the club. It as a small, smelly bathroom with toilet paper, cigarette butts, paper towels and stray hairs littered all over the floor and counter top. Teresa studied her face in the mirror as she combed her hair. Maybe it was just the fluorescent light, but her skin looked sallow and dead with dark rings around her eyes.

The toilet flushed behind her and Karen emerged. She washed her hands and reapplied her lipstick, then dug in her purse for awhile.

"I brought us something," Karen said as she searched in her purse. Her hand stopped moving and closed around something. She looked up at Teresa and smiled. Her hand opened to two joints sitting in her palm.

Teresa laughed. Karen lit them and they leaned against the wall of the bathroom slowly, silently smoking. Some women, mostly club employees, walked in and glanced at them. No one said anything. Teresa's head was throbbing and she realized she was going to get a headache from this. She scowled at the smoke curling in the air towards the door.

"Do you think they can smell this out there?"

"Who cares." Karen threw the remains of her joint into the toilet. Teresa coughed and the pain in her head pressed hard against her temples. She threw hers into the toilet and Karen flushed. They walked back out into the night of the club.

"Hey, baby," a sailor said and reached out and brushed Teresa's butt as she walked by. She wanted to lash out at him but just tensed her body in anger and kept on walking.

Greg and Myrna had returned to the table. Teresa sat down in her chair and leaned against the backrest. She closed her eyes and tried to breathe deeply to ease the throbbing in her head. When she opened her eyes again she saw her.

It was the girl from the bridge. Her image flickered across the glass of a mirror mounted on the wall opposite Teresa. The glare of the strobe lights washed out the image at frequent intervals. But it kept returning.

The girl was dressed in a bikini similar to the one most of the other women wore. It was gold and high-cut and very brief. She was dancing on one of the pedestals around the dance floor. She didn't look happy, she didn't look scared she just looked. No emotion. Her body didn't show any emotion either. Bared to the eyes of the men around her, she barely moved in time to the music.

Teresa felt sick as she watched the girl. She can't be more than fourteen, she thought, although the girl was made up to look older. A man, one of the waiters, walked up to the girl and helped her off her pedestal. Teresa turned away from the mirror and searched the crowd for the girl.

She found her by the bar with the waiter. They stood in front of a very pale man perched on a bar stool. The man slid off the stool with difficulty and slowly, deliberately closed his arm around the girl's waist. She jerked as if to run, but the waiter behind her kept her in her place.

The man might have been Navy, although he was very fat. He was fairly well-dressed in a blue, striped suit and pleated blue pants. A light mustache dripped around his mouth, which was slightly open to help him breathe. Light blonde-gray hair fell across his eyes. Teresa tried to guess what age he was but couldn't tell. Maybe thirties. Maybe forties. He gave the waiter some money and slowly made his way out the door, holding the girl.

Teresa watched intently until they were gone. Then she laid her head on the table and tried not to cry. Her head hurt so badly it felt like it was pounding against the hard wood of the table. She finally looked up. None of her friends seemed to have seen what she had. None of them seemed to have noticed her.

Teresa reached for her glass and poured some mojo from the pitcher. It was warm and sweet. She drank it quickly. She was still depressed, so she poured another.

The image of a woman in the mirror caught her eye. It was an older woman, overweight and wrinkled. Teresa wondered if she had started out like the young girl. This woman danced the same way, emotionlessly. Teresa looked around and realized that all the women danced the same way. She studied each woman individually, looking for something in their eyes, their painted lips that would tell her something about them. Then she made up stories about them, how they had gotten where they were.

It depressed her even more. And it upset her because she could only sit and watch. Less than an hour had passed. Or maybe it was more than an hour. Teresa wasn't sure. She was caught up in the intertwining threads, the net of all the women's lives.

She was surprised to find a San Miguel beer in her hand. Had she ordered a beer? She didn't even like San Miguel.

"Where's that photographer?" Greg complained. "It's been an hour already."

Karen murmured something, in agreement it seemed, because she was nodding. The other two ignored Greg. They wouldn't worry about the photo until they were ready to leave.

Teresa stopped drinking. There didn't seem any more point. It certainly wasn't doing her any good. She had a pounding headache and she was feeling sick to her stomach. Dave asked her to dance but she declined.

Lights flashed around her and people moved in and out of focus as they passed by to go to the dance floor or the bathroom or outside or wherever. Teresa wasn't sure anymore. She didn't really try to figure any of it out either. Thinking about any of it only made her feel worse, she decided. The glasses and pitchers around her kept changing places, disappearing and reappearing with each arrival of the waiter.

"We should get going soon," Dave remarked during a slow, and somewhat quiet, song. "It's getting kind of late."

"What time is it?" Karen asked.

"Almost one."

"What time did we get here?"

"I don't know." Dave thought about it for a minute. "I guess about nine, nine-thirty."

Four hours, or around there, Teresa thought. We've been here four hours. She felt thick-headed.

The photographer reappeared. No apologies. Nothing. He just held out the pictures to them and said something to Greg.

"What?" Greg exclaimed. He motioned to Teresa. "Teresa, come here."

She pushed herself out of her seat and stumbled over to him.

"What?" Her tongue felt thick and dry as she spoke.

"He says he wants eighty pesos for these pictures."

"So?"

"So see if you can talk him down."

75

Teresa pulled herself up and looked at the man. "Eighty ba ang hinihingi ninyo?"

"Oo."

"Fifty."

The man shook his head adamantly. "Eighty." He held up the pictures in his hand. "Kung ayaw ninyo ito, itatapon ko na lang." And he pretended to pitch the pictures over his shoulder to make his point.

Teresa was tired. "Oh fuck it! Just give the man his eighty." She pressed her fingers against her temples and felt the throbbing in her head. Greg looked at her in surprise then opened his wallet and gave the man a twenty. The others started digging in their wallets.

Teresa stumbled back to her chair and pulled a twenty out of her purse. The man took his money and threw the pictures on the table. Teresa reached for one and shoved it in her purse without looking at it. The queasy feeling in her stomach was intensifying and moving up her throat.

"Excuse me," she mumbled and hurriedly pushed away from the table. She teetered to the bathroom and into a stall. The floor of the stall was wet and it smelled of urine. Teresa rested her hands on her knees and leaned over, her face hanging above the dirty white toilet bowl. Her hair kept getting in her face and she kept pushing it behind her ears. Nothing happened.

She leaned against the wall of the stall and tried to relax. Her stomach was churning but it seemed for now that she was not going to throw up. She still felt too sick to leave the bathroom though.

Noise from the club spilled in as someone walked in the bathroom door. Two people. Club dancers. Teresa could see them through the cracks in the door of the stall. They lit up cigarettes and stood in front of the sink talking and fixing their hair and makeup.

"Narinig mo ba ang nangyari kay Carmelita?"

"Carmelita?"

"Iyon bata. Iyon bagong bata."

Teresa tensed against the wall of the stall. They were talking about the girl. Carmelita. The little baby of a girl she'd seen dancing in the mirror.

"Ano?"

"E, alam mo iyon kumuha sa kanya? Iyon mataba?"

"Oo."

"E, pinatay."

"Ano?" The woman dropped her cigarette.

Teresa closed her eyes. Her hands closed into tight fists and the nails of her fingers dug into each palm. Dead.

"Anong nangyari?"

"Ang narinig ko lang ay dinala sa Olongapo General Hospital. Internal bleeding. At pinick-up nang police iyon mamang mataba. Manslaughter daw."

"Nako." Silence. "Ang bata pa naman."

They stubbed their cigarettes out and threw them in the trashcan. One of the women adjusted the bottom of her bikini. The door opened. Music rushed in and was quickly muffled by the closing door.

Teresa stood alone in the bathroom against the wall of the stall. She couldn't even remember the face of the girl. Sniffling, she reached in her purse for a Kleenex and came up with the picture instead.

It was mostly gray. A cheap and fuzzy photo. Everyone grouped around the table, smiling self-consciously. Her hand went limp and she let the picture flutter into the toilet bowl.

Then she threw up. Everything seemed to be pushing out of her. Her stomach, the whole area around her waist, her chest tightened and pushed. She heaved and heaved into the dirty white bowl. It seemed as if she would never be able to take a breath.

When it finally stopped, she stood shakily over the bowl

and flushed. Whirlpools of water carried the waste down, down and away. It's going to the river now, where the little boys swim, Teresa thought.

A Modern Parable: The Elections in San Lazaro

Eduardo Alegado, Eddie to his friends and associates, was snatched from the small bar he frequented a few days before the elections. The two gunmen, who didn't even bother to mask their faces, ran into the bar waving their pistols and dragged Eddie from a table where he was having a beer while soliciting donations for his campaign.

After the initial shouts of surprise, the place was eerily quiet. Eddie walked out with his head up and "trailing the smell of death after him" as Mang Apo later described it. Others argued that it was just the smell of the beer, which had spilled on Eddie when the gunmen had hauled him out of his chair. No one mentioned the possibility that Eddie had urinated in his pants. It wouldn't be a very honorable way to remember a man who had been a faithful Catholic and a good friend.

The gunmen fled in a shiny orange Tamaraw jeepney but not before shooting a round off at a policeman who had run up to investigate.

When the other police officers arrived Eddie's friends and the other bar patrons were milling helplessly outside the bar. No one had bothered to help the downed policeman. He was in a bloody mess on the sidewalk.

"Who were the gunmen?" Officer Mamaril cried.

We don't know, was the reply. We have never seen them before.

"Can you describe them?" The officer was on the verge of hysteria.

No, everyone agreed. It all happened so quickly.

"Please," he begged. "We will protect you."

But the bar patrons looked at the body of the policeman on the sidewalk and shook their heads.

Without evidence, the police blamed the Communists for "carrying out this heinous act in order to disrupt the democratic electoral process" and hunted for the perpetrators, whom they had no description of. They picked up a farmer for suspiciously loitering in front of the bar and a teacher for suspected Communist affiliations.

They were forced to let the teacher go when her lawyer pointed out that even if she was a Communist, which she was not, she had committed no violent or subversive acts. The farmer they let out after a week with two black eyes and a bruised body. They said he had fallen down some stairs.

They never found the gunmen. The day after the elections, from which two other candidates withdrew, a rice sack was deposited outside the police station, with Eddie's severely beaten body inside.

All Souls

All Souls' Eve Peping woke up with a start and hit his head on the marble tomb. In a panic, he groped through the air until his left hand touched fire. "Ow!" He jerked his hand back. The pain shocked him out of the nightmare of the tomb and brought him back to the candlelit evening. With the side of his face against the cool, smooth marble, he sucked on the two burned fingers while he tried to make out the shadowy figures of his family seated on the grass around him.

Peping shifted his weight so that the marble touched and cooled his back. It was a humid, hot night even out in the cemetery on the edge of town. Peping wondered if the candles burning on all the gravestones and tombs and inside all the mausoleums tonight were adding to the heat.

Long, thick, yellow candles burned in front of the tomb Peping leaned against. It was his grandfather's tomb. This lifesize, rectangular container of his grandfather's bones and dust stopped just short of the earth from which it was raised by a concrete slab. Just around the corner from where Peping rested, the candles illuminated the nameplate on the tomb, and provided light for those who were keeping vigil.

Music came from the transistor radio Peping's mother had brought along. Peping was too far away to hear anything other than the bass. One-and-two-and-three-and-four. The beat never wavered or changed. It sounded like his sisters' taste in music.

Peping's mother was crocheting something—a tablecloth or

maybe curtains—by the meager light of the candles, his older sister intently reading a magazine. Their father sat nearby playing cards and drinking rum with some of the men. Gloria, Peping's younger sister, had left an hour ago, saying that she was going to look for some of her girlfriends. Peping was sure that she was really going to look for Carlito.

"O, Peping!" one of the men called out. "Are you awake?"

"Come here Peping!" His father motioned him over.

Peping uncurled his legs and stood up. His legs were stiff and sore, as if the nightmare had been true and he'd lain trapped in the tomb. He massaged his legs until they felt warm and alive again, then walked carefully around his grandmother kneeling in front of the grave and squatted beside his father.

His father and the other men were playing cards, but not very seriously. One of the men told a joke and the others laughed, spilling their cards onto their laps. A half-empty bottle of rum was passed around and Peping took a sip.

It was good rum and slid smoothly down his throat. The warmth and tingling of it spread through his belly. He drank some more.

The others gave up the bottle for lost and opened another one. A few cigarettes were lit and mingled with the rum-soaked air around the men. Peping rocked back and forth on his feet. The men took up their cards again.

Gloria returned. Their mother was talking to her, and she was responding sulkily. His other sister, the older one, was still reading her magazine and ignoring the two beside her. Peping looked Gloria over carefully with the suspicion of a jealous, possessive brother. His eyes strayed from her slightly mussed hair, down to her shirt and pants. A missing button, an untucked portion of her shirt, a stain on the pants—all of these he looked for but did not find.

Peping's eyes wandered back to his grandmother kneeling patiently in front of the grave, the only one keeping the religious vigil. One of the candles had burned down. His grandmother lit another one and tilted it to let a few drops of wax drip onto the marble. She pushed the candle into the small mound of soft wax and held it until the wax cooled. Then she continued softly praying

A few words of the prayer drifted over. "... Espiritu Santo." It conjured memories of kneeling in front of the family altar with the statue of the Santo Niño and reciting Spanish prayers that he didn't understand. Always there were candles that flickered like the ones on the tomb. And the Santo Niño wavered in the heat from the candles just as the streaks in the marble tomb wavered now. The streaks mixed with the smoke and looked like a spirit rising from the grave of his grandfather.

Peping pulled a pack of cigarettes from his shirt pocket. He took one out and tapped the tip of it against his palm as if to pack the tobacco in tighter. "Tatay," he whispered as he nudged his father. "Tatay." His father looked up from his hand of cards. Peping held out the unlit cigarette. His father took his cigarette out of his mouth and held the tip against Peping's cigarette until a slender strand of smoke rose from it.

Peping sat back on his heels and took short drags of the cigarette. Mostly he just watched the smoke rise from it. "This Nonoy ...!" his father exclaimed in mock anger. He was losing but enjoying himself. "I'm going to lose all my money to him!" The others laughed. A woman keeping vigil by the neighboring gravesite frowned in disapproval at them. She must think we're really gambling, Peping thought.

He took a few more sips from the bottle of rum and leaned closer in order to get a good look at his father's hand. A queen of hearts, a king of spades, not much else. He took a long sip from the bottle and thought about it. "Tatay ...," he said, whispering some hints to his father.

His father smiled and tried one of the plays. It worked.

Nonoy grumbled good-naturedly about it being unfair to receive help. Peping's father smacked Peping on the thigh. "That's why this boy made it into college." Nonoy asked if that was the kind of thing Peping learned in college and everyone laughed.

Peping lost his balance and fell back on the ground. This made the others laugh even harder and his father mockingly waved the empty rum bottle in front of his face. The game stopped while another bottle of rum was passed around.

Peping remained lying on the grass. He stared at the black shapes of the clouds. At night the clouds looked heavy the way they moved darkly across the sky.

His father nudged him in the leg. Peping saw that his father was offering him some rum. He shook his head and waved the bottle away. The cloud shapes captivated him in the way they slowly changed and moved in and out of each other.

"Look at that," Peping said to the others. He pointed up at the cloud that was almost directly above him. "Doesn't it look like Bebs Balboa?" he said, referring to a popular movie actress. The others looked up at the cloud. Nonoy finally said that he couldn't make out Bebs' face in that cloud. Peping said that he wasn't talking about Bebs' face. The others laughed.

A few who were drunk laughed so hard that they had to lie down like Peping. Nonoy pointed out another cloud and said it looked like Angie Alarcon, the popular singer. The others asked what part of Angie and proceeded to guess.

A wisp of smoke from Peping's cigarette curled towards a cloud. In Peping's eyes, the smoke and cloud merged into one so that he couldn't tell if the smoke had dissipated or become part of the shifting cloud pattern. He stared at the cloud intently. "It looks like grandfather," he whispered.

The comment startled Peping's father, who followed his son's gaze up to the cloud. "It does," he agreed in surprise.

He lay down on the grass beside Peping to get a better look at the cloud that resembled his father.

An awkward quiet lay over the group as they looked up at the clouds. Peping sensed that the others were seeing things too; perhaps images and fragments of the dead stirred in the backs of their minds as they did in his mind tonight. The black, smooth underbelly of a cloud reminded Peping of a fish he had seen his great grandfather clean once when he was a very little boy.

Peping's father broke the silence. "You know, when I as a little boy ...." He reminisced. "Do you all remember Mang Tanda?" his father asked the others. Grunts of assent, small smiles showed they remembered the man whom they had as small boys nicknamed Mang Tanda. They had thought it a clever play on the word matanda: old. He had been Mang Tanda to Peping and his generation too. The neighborhood had joked that he would live forever until he died two years ago.

Mang Tanda and the clouds that moved overhead. The clouds were slow and dark like the old man had been. A cloud ahead seemed to hesitate, or maybe the hesitation was just in Peping's mind. A small grunt, an almost-laugh, escaped from him. It was so like the hesitation of Mang Tanda, his grandfather, and his great grandfather in their old age.

Peping sat up and held his knees close to him, absently rubbing his jaw across a kneecap. His father was staring intently at the tomb and the back of Peping's grandmother outlined by the burning candles. He had the look of someone whose eyes had rested on something or someone he didn't really see.

Large clouds of smoke rose from the many burning candles. That kind of cheap, yellow candle always gave out a lot of smoke. Peping wondered how his grandmother could breathe with the smoke all around her, settling on her skin, her hair, burning her eyes.

"When I was younger, during the war, our house burned

down," his father said as he stared at the smoke. "Your grandfather and I tried to put it out, but it was no use because there wasn't enough water." He reached a hand out as if to touch the long-ago house. "Your grandmother sat in front of the house, just like that, the whole time, watching it burn." Peping's father watched the house dissolve into smoke again before him.

Peping suddenly remembered a time when he had been smoking secretly in the back of the house, squeezed in between the house and the back wall that separated them from the canal. His father had caught him and given him a beating not because he was smoking but because he had carelessly thrown the matches down without checking if they were out or if they had landed among some leaves or grass. Ever since then it had become habit for him to ask his father to light his cigarettes.

Peping smiled and pulled the pack of cigarettes out of his shirt pocket. He picked a cigarette out and held it before his father who automatically fished in his pocket for a lighter and lit it. Peping sat hunched over his knees breathing out puffs of smoke and staring at the tomb that had brought him out here tonight to the edge of town with his family, among some men who should be watching over their own relatives' graves but didn't want to. None of them wanted to be alone tonight or locked in a somber vigil with their families.

Supposedly they came out here to pay their respects to the dead. But Peping didn't feel respectful or religious among the graves. Surrounded by people he and the others around him had known so well, he felt dragged down with his own mortality.

So what? he thought. His accomplishments, his twinges of guilt at his feelings toward his sister, his memories of the past—all seemed so ephemeral and transparent when confronted here with the end of life and their trivial attempts to remember those past lives.

Peping sighed and took a long sip from the bottle of rum. Maybe he was just drunk in the wrong place tonight. Maybe not. Peping thought he could see in the others the same thing he was feeling. Something communicated by an uneasy look in the eyes, by the need to huddle together and forget where they were through the many shared bottles.

"It wasn't like this when I was younger," he whispered to himself. In the silence he watched the cigarette burn down in his hands. He stubbed it out quickly and flicked it away.

"It gets like this when you're older," his father's voice whispered back, surprising him. "Unless you're like your grandmother." His father sat up. Peping followed him.

The others had already sat up and were whispering among themselves. Peping's grandmother was still in front of the grave only now she was sitting, instead of kneeling, in an attitude of prayer. Peping thought for a moment that maybe she was asleep, but she was shifted her seating slightly, dispelling his doubts.

"Maybe she is bothered by these things," his father continued, masking a fact that was too frightening, too unnerving to face with the general, painless term "these things." "But, she doesn't show it. When our house burned down your grandfather cried, but your grandmother, she said it was a sign we should leave. So, we left Manila and didn't come back until the war was over." He paused and looked at Peping for a moment but was too unsure of himself and quickly looked away.

Peping nudged a card that lay face down in front of him. He swatted it around. It didn't go very far; it kept getting caught on blades of grass. Peping laid a hand on it and tried to guess what it was before he turned it over. A queen ... of hearts. Wrong. It was a three. A three of spades.

He passed the card to his father thinking it was his. The others started passing their cards back to his father. It was almost morning and no one was interested in the card game anymore.

A rooster crowed although daylight hadn't yet broken through the murky grayness. The other men suddenly became animated. Their voices rose as they rose from their seats on the lawn. A few groans and grunts, good-natured slaps on the back, and the clanking of glass bottles accompanied their slow exodus from the cemetery.

Their noises blended into the steadily increasing noise of hundreds of bodies moving. More roosters crowed in chorus. The lights from the candles blinked out as they were extinguished. People packed up their belongings. Jeepneys honked along the road in front of the cemetery trying to attract passengers on their way home. "Later, Nonoy!" his father called out and the men were gone, dispersed across the cemetery to their separate families.

Peping's grandmother called the family together for one last prayer. They crowded around the altar of misshapen candles that were still trailing wisps of smoke. Peping was kneeling behind his sister Gloria. He glanced down at her pants leg and noticed grass stains near the cuff. She may have gotten it from sitting on the grass by the tomb, he thought. And then maybe not.

The sun was peeping out above the rows of shops in front of the cemetery. "... now and forever, Amen." The prayers concluded, they crossed themselves, and stood up to leave. Peping's father helped his grandmother from her place in front of the tomb.

Peping licked his right index finger and thumb, bent down, and squeezed a still-smoking candlewick between his fingers. There was a quick sensation of heat and then the smoking stopped. He leaned his hand against the tomb as he stood back up. It still felt cold. Peping left with the sense that the tomb, that cold, hard, smooth object was lodged in his belly.

Balikbayan

Ruth woke up in the early morning with the top sheet wound tightly around her feet and lower legs. She felt trapped. Of course, she had done it to herself, with all her tossing and turning during the night.

She thought her toes had gone numb. She couldn't feel them, but it was hard to feel or move anything through the tightly wrapped sheet. She didn't unwind the sheet. Instead, she lay on the thin mattress breathing in the musty air and watching the grayness of early morning disappear in the shafts of sunlight poking through the curtains.

Ruth felt a prickling sensation on the back of her neck. She shivered and turned to look into the eyes of the Jesus with his heart in his hands. The statue sat on the bedside table watching her. Even in the daytime, when the tropical sun streamed through the window to cast its burning light on everything, the statue appeared to breathe. It made her uncomfortable and she wanted to turn it to the wall, but she was afraid to.

She raised herself up on one elbow and, with her free hand, crossed herself while staring at the statue. Faint sounds of people talking and pots banging crept under the crack in the bedroom door. Downstairs, the screen door to the kitchen closed with a loud slap. Ruth finally disentangled her feet from the sheets and threw a faded, red bathrobe on, her eyes never straying from the Jesus with his heart in his hands.

She walked down the hallway, passing the empty, mostly unused rooms as quickly as possible. They made her nervous, as if her grandmother could be hiding somewhere in the musty darkness of them. It was a feeling that had haunted her since her grandmother had died a week ago. Ruth was thankful when she finally got downstairs into the glow of dawn and the smell of eggs and coffee.

She stepped briskly through the living and dining rooms, past the first kitchen, where all the food was stored, into the second kitchen, where the cooking was really done. The spatter of sizzling eggs and the warm smell of rice frying in garlic filled the small, crowded room. One of the large golden-brown cats brushed against her legs as Aunt Lita shooed it out of the kitchen with a broom.

"Ruthie! You finally woke up," Aunt Irma greeted her cheerfully. She sat on the footstool by the sink snipping the ends off of pea pods.

"Did you have a good sleep?" Auntie Lita asked. She was struggling to put the bag of chicken feed away on the top shelf of the cabinet.

"Yes," Ruth said. She realized Auntie Lita couldn't reach the shelf because Aunt Irma had the stool. "I'll put that away." Ruth took the bag away from her and placed it on the top shelf. Aunt Lita went to wash her hands in the sink.

"Breakfast is ready," Aunt Virgie announced.

Ruth helped her put the eggs and rice on serving plates and they carried them into the dining room. The sun shone strongly through the windows. The aunts discussed business and the day's plans as they ate.

"The lawyer said he could meet us on Tuesday at ten. Can you get off work then?"

"I think so. Did he mention anything about the land in Parañaque?"

"No."

"I'm going to leave right after the mass so I can get the house ready before the guests arrive. Lourdes's son will give me a ride."

They talked quickly and ate quickly. They didn't believe in wasting time. Ruth knew that while she lay sleeping they had been busily bringing the house back to life: folding clothes, making notes for themselves and the maids, feeding the chickens, and cooking breakfast. They cast disapproving but kindly glances at her, unwashed and swathed in her red bathrobe.

"The funeral is in three hours. Father Saguisig will pick us up at nine-thirty and take us to the church." Auntie Virgie stopped to take a sip of her coffee. "I'm having Claring iron your new, white dress, so you can wear it to the mass today." Ruth sighed. Auntie Virgie and the other aunts wanted to make sure that she didn't try to wear anything inappropriate.

Their coffee finished, the aunts excused themselves and scattered off to different corners of the house on their various errands. Claring and the two younger maids sat down to their breakfast. They ate quickly to avoid the disapproval of the aunts. Ruth deliberately ate slowly, and they finished before she did.

She took her dishes to the sink then wandered into the living room to read the paper. One of the maids dusted and swept around her. Auntie Virgie brought some flowers in from the garden.

"Ruthie." She stopped in front of Ruth. "Aren't you going to take your shower before we go to church?"

"Yes." Ruth stared at the paper in her hands. "But, I want to read the paper first."

"Okay." Aunt Virgie walked into the first kitchen and Ruth could hear her searching through the cabinets for a vase.

Ruth leafed through the paper, scanning the headlines. "American kidnapped in Beirut." "NPA ambush kills three." "China delegation to meet with Agri Minister." Relatives banged and called at the gate. The noise jolted Ruth back into the world of her aunts.

"Ruthie! Go take your shower!" Aunt Virgie yelled from the kitchen.

"I am!" Ruth yelled back irritably.

She ran to the upstairs bathroom to get ready for the funeral. When she returned to her room, a white dress was waiting under the infinitely patient eyes of the Jesus. It was a knee-length, off-white dress of piña fabric with intricate embroidery of flowers and curlicues, and smaller versions of the classic Filipino butterfly sleeves.

She sighed and slipped it on. It was cool and light and sheer. Ruth searched through her still unpacked bags for a slip to wear with it. She undressed and dressed again and looked at herself in the mirror.

She did look different. It was because of the dress. The dress was sweet and innocent. She looked as if she were still the obedient, respectful girl who would grow up to take care of her aunts and grandmother in their old age.

Those of course were the very reasons she had left and disappointed them. But, she hadn't changed much. Maybe, Ruth thought, that was why she had felt so guilty and why she had come back after ten years.

"Ruthie," Claring whispered as she tapped lightly on the door.

"Yes?"

"Ma'am wants you to come down as soon as you're ready."

The message probably was from Aunt Virgie, in which case she meant now not later.

She picked up her brush and angrily ran it through her hair. The brush caught painfully on a knot of hair. She gently, carefully worked it through. Her grandmother would have done the same. She used to love to brush Ruth's long, black hair. Ruth lay the brush on the dresser.

She didn't want to go to her grandmother's funeral. But there was no way out of it. She turned around and reached for her white shoes poking out from under the bed. As she turned back to the dresser mirror, the eyes of the Jesus with his heart in his hands caught her eye. Ruth shivered and quickly looked away.

"Ruthie." Claring tapped on the door again. Aunt Virgie apparently had sent her back upstairs. Ruth didn't say anything. She fumbled with the straps of her shoes. "Ruthie, Ma'am wants you to come down soon."

"Okay! Okay!" Ruth said in exasperation. She grabbed the doorknob and pulled the door open, startling Claring who was still standing on the other side.

Claring scurried down the stairs ahead of her. The voices from the living room grew louder as another group of relatives arrived and were greeted by everyone. Ruth couldn't understand why they didn't just go to the church instead of waiting around for her and her aunts. She wished they would leave. The thought of having to face their inquisitive, understanding eyes only added to her anger.

Ruth walked down the stairs and joined her relatives. Aunt Virgie grabbed her by the hand and led her to Father Saguisig. "Father, this is Ruth, Eva's daughter," Aunt Virgie announced enthusiastically. "She is balikbayan. Back home from the States." Ruth's hand lay imprisoned in hers as she made her proclamation.

Father Saguisig smiled brightly at Ruth and Aunt Virgie, who was smiling triumphantly. Ruth managed a quick, insincere smile. Father Saguisig didn't seem to notice. Ruth relaxed a bit when Aunt Virgie finally let go of her hand to attend to business in some other part of the house.

"I never met your mother, but I have heard a lot about her," Father said politely.
Ruth nodded. "I've heard a lot about her too," she said coldly. Her mother had died when Ruth was four and she didn't remember her. But her aunts and her grandmother had told her many stories.

Father Saguisig seemed surprised by her comment. He scanned the room, as if looking for help. He looked back at Ruth. "Your Aunt Virgie tells me that your grandmother threw a party for you when you returned."

Ruth nodded. "Yes," she said, again coldly. It had been like the homecoming of the prodigal granddaughter.

"She must have been very glad to have you back."

"Well, I am glad to be back for vacation." She emphasized the last word. "But I will be leaving ...." Aunt Lita and Aunt Virgie scurried up to join them.

"We are just waiting for Irma and then we'll be ready to go."

"Ruth and I were just talking about the party her grandmother threw for her."

Ruth's aunts nodded understandingly. "You know, she died that evening." Aunt Virgie lowered her voice to a hiss. "She was so happy to have Ruthie back." Both aunts shook their heads sadly. Ruth clenched her teeth. Her lips pressed together into a thin line. Aunt Virgie didn't notice and patted her sympathetically on the back.

Aunt Irma finally finished getting ready and they rode to the church with Father Saguisig. Ruth sat quietly in the back seat, squeezed in with her aunts, and watched the jeepneys and cars fighting for space on the road.

By the time they arrived at the church, she was feeling a little less angry. Instead she felt tired and lethargic. They entered the church, the same one she had attended many times as a child, and sat in the reserved front pew. The casket sat in front of them, but Ruth kept her eyes focused on her hands lying in her lap. Aunt Virgie sat to her right, and Aunts Irma and Lita sat to her left like some kind of protective barrier around her. Ruth could hear them shifting uncomfortably in their seats and fanning themselves with their intricately embroidered fans.

The pianist began playing and Father Saguisig marched

down the aisle with two altar boys. The mass was in Tagalog. Ruth had forgotten how long it had been since she had heard a Tagalog mass. Even in Manila masses were in English half the time. But the aunts had insisted on a traditional funeral.

Ruth stared at the sheet of paper with the order of the mass printed on it. "Hanggang Doon Kay Bathala Si Gng. Ma. Lucita B. Gutierrez" was printed at the top. "Until Mrs. Maria Lucita B. Gutierrez is with God." God and Bathala. Bathala, prehispanic god of thunder, maker of the first man and woman, creator of the islands, had merged with the western God of Son and Holy Spirit. Ruth found it funny.

"Hanggang doon kay Bathala si Ginang Maria Lucita Gutierrez," intoned the woman reader at the lectern in the conclusion to her eulogy. The crowd echoed the words.

The heat and light from the early morning sun spread into the church and settled over the altar and the pews giving everything and everyone a warm, copper glow. It was unbearably hot. All the bodies gathered in the church were adding a heavy, musky smell to the already humid air. Ruth felt heavy and faint.

"Auntie Virgie," she whispered urgently. Her mouth and throat were so dry she felt she would choke. "Auntie Virgie, I don't feel well. I'm going to get some fresh air."

"Are you okay?" Aunt Virgie said, very concerned. She always became worried when the slightest thing was wrong. "I can go with you."

"No ...." Ruth tried to swallow. "No, I'll be all right. I just need some fresh air."

She clutched her purse and walked unsteadily down the side aisle. Vaguely recognizable faces looked up at her as she passed. Finally, she reached the outside of the church and heaved herself down onto the grimy steps. The air outside was as hot and heavy as inside. Ruth looked around for a vendor selling soda or something else to drink.

"Ay! Stand up! Stand up!" A nearly-toothless, sun-baked old lady sat beside the church door waving her hands and berating Ruth. "Stand up! Stand up!" The woman urged Ruth. "Your dress!" Ruth stood up in bewilderment. She looked with dismay at her soiled dress. The old woman shook her head sadly at Ruth's carelessness.

The strains of the organ and "Lamb of God" came from inside. "Lamb of God you take away the sins of the world," the crowd sang, slightly off-key. "Have mercy on us."

A soft scent drifted from the shallow basket that lay in front of the old woman. Strands of small, delicate, white sampaguitas lay wilting inside. The woman noticed Ruth looking at them and held up in her cracked, worn hands one of the better looking strands. "For the shrine of the Mother of God? Only two pesos." Ruth fished ten pesos out of her purse and bought five strands of sampaguita.

Communion was beginning as she reentered the church. To the right of the door, hidden in a dark alcove, was the shrine of the Mother. She stood on a high pedestal serenely looking beyond the pagan offerings of her worshippers. Small, yellow candles flickered at her feet and strands of sampaguita lay around her neck.

Ruth stood up on the tips of her toes and, using the railing around the statue for support, placed two strands of small, white flowers around the neck of the Mother of God. She felt ridiculous. It was a waste of flowers. What did the statue care about sampaguitas?

Ruth stepped out of the alcove and watched the people filing back to their pews after receiving communion. She crept down the side aisle back to the front pew where her aunts sat. They had apparently finished saying their communion prayers and sat in their seats waiting for the mass to continue.

Ruth leaned over and placed a necklace of sampaguitas around Aunt Virgie's neck. Aunt Virgie turned to her in surprise. Ruth placed a necklace of sampaguitas each around

Aunt Lita's and Aunt Irma's necks. They looked confused. Aunt Lita held the sampaguitas to her nose and breathed in the sweet smell. Ruth smiled at them. She felt a little like the Jesus with his heart in his hands who trusts that no one will hurt or ignore it.